NO WAY TO DIE
A MING DYNASTY MYSTERY

P. A. De Voe

NO WAY TO DIE

A Ming Dynasty Mystery

P.A. DE VOE

Drum
Tower
Press

Printed in the United States of America

Publisher's Note This is a work of fiction. Names, characters, places, and incidents either are the product of the author's imagination or are used fictitiously, and any resemblance to actual persons, living or dead, business establishments, events, or locales is entirely coincidental.

Cover design by P.A. De Voe

Published by: Drum Tower Press, LLC

165 Bon Chateau Drive

Saint Louis, Missouri 63141-6081

http://padevoe.com/?page_id=177

LCCN 201990782

ISBN 978-1-942667-11-7 (paperback)

ISBN 978-1-942667-12-4 (e-book)

To discover more stories about Imperial China, visit padevoe.com

An incessant banging woke Xiang-hua. Lifting herself up on one elbow and staring out into the darkened room, she strained to hear what was happening. Her father's deep, sleepy voice rolled through the hallway. He ordered his servant to find out who had come to their home so early in the morning and to let them enter only in the case of a true emergency.

Time slowed in the wake of this order. As she waited, Xiang-hua rose, lit a lantern, and checked her medical bag to make sure she had adequate necessities in case the stranger had come for her services. In her brief experience as the only available fully trained women's doctor, she had already learned to expect families to seek her care no matter the time.

She stepped over to the neat piles of books and supplies on her desk, then removed the sheet of rice paper, brush, ink, and ink stone she would need to write a prescription.

As she carefully slipped the items into her bag, the family's maid entered the room. The elderly servant had been with the Xin family years before Xiang-hua's birth and had cared for her ever since. However, now the maid spoke with her head bowed slightly, avoiding Xiang-hua's eyes and speaking to her midriff. "You are needed immediately, Young Miss. There has been a death at the herbalist's home, and you've been sent for."

Xiang-hua pursed her lips. "A death? Why am I needed? There is nothing I can do in such a situation."

The older servant's gaze never rose, and, although her face remained impassive, Xiang-hua noted a slight tightening around her mouth. "Your father wants to speak to you."

The woman's bowed head and unusually circumspect demeanor piqued Xiang-hua's curiosity. While always respectful, the family maid was typically much more familiar with her young mistress. Now wasn't the time to inquire further, however.

"Of course. Get my day dress."

Xiang-hua immediately changed into her serviceable and sensible work clothes: long, loose-legged pants of celadon-dyed cotton and a darker green tunic with flowers of the same emerald hue woven into the fabric. Over these, she threw on a peach-colored, heavy, cotton robe that reached to just below her knees.

Dashing out the door and down the hall, she soon arrived at the main reception area. A man wearing a short jacket and leggings tied just below the knee sat in quiet conversation with her father. She recognized him as a local volunteer of the town's security team.

Her father, still dressed in his informal house robe, looked up as she entered the room. "Xiang-hua, come in," he said, tension underlaying his otherwise calm voice.

Her throat tightened. She moved forward and stood before her father, hands tucked into the opposite sleeves of her robe. Willing a composure she didn't feel, she waited for him to explain the situation. She didn't have long to wait.

"There has been a terrible accident at the herbalist's house," he continued somberly. "A peddler found a man lying outside on the ground. Dead."

Xiang-hua nodded, almost relieved. A tragedy, of course, but not something that would involve her. First, while a male doctor could treat men and women, a female doctor could only attend to female patients, never men. No matter how well trained and experienced she might be. To do so would be an extraordinary breach of social standards. Second, the man was dead; there was nothing she could do anyway.

As she absorbed this information, Xiang-hua's brow wrinkled in consternation. She was no closer to understanding why this fellow had come to their house or why her father asked for her.

Her father's hand rubbed the lapels of his robe as if smoothing the already flawless material. After a silent moment, he nodded toward the messenger. "From what he just told me, Zhong, the security team's leader, believes the death is not from natural causes. He needs a coroner to officially examine the body. For documentation to be sent to the courts." He paused again, as if lost in thought.

After alternately crunching then straightening his robe, he continued: "He wants you to come and perform the coroner's duty in this case."

Xiang-hua blinked. *A coroner? Zhong wants me to examine a dead man, looking for possible criminality?*

"Now, I don't want you to think you have to do this," he quickly amended. "This isn't an official court investigation. Yet. Therefore, a coroner isn't strictly required. As head of the security team, Zhong could examine the body himself. But he's being proactive. Apparently, he's sure he's going to have to send in an official death report to the provincial court."

"Isn't Granny Ao-po our town's coroner?" she asked.

Granny Ao-po, a midwife, was widowed and well past child-bearing age. Often the coroner was a woman, not a man, who had some connection to an informal branch of medicine. Nevertheless, it was unusual to have someone with Xiang-hua's level of medical training perform such a lowly service.

"Granny Ao-po's not available." Her father nodded at the security team's messenger. "Which is why Zhong wants you. If he has to send in a report to the provincial magistrate, Zhong wants to be sure there are no errors."

He again quickly added: "I'm passing on the security team leader's request, but, as I've said, you don't have to go." His repetitions and uncommonly flustered speech weren't lost on her. Clearly, her father held mixed emotions about this situation and her potential role in it.

The messenger leaned slightly forward in his chair, as if about to say something, but then leaned back and merely waited for her reply.

Now the maid's odd behavior made sense. As part of a medical family, Xiang-hua's role as a doctor was accepted and respected by all. But a coroner was a different matter entirely. Because they dealt with those who died under suspicious or violent circumstances, coroners occupied dangerous and undesirable jobs of low social standing. People who died before their time left behind angry spirits who were capable of bringing harm to the living, especially to those who handled their remains. No one, not even the head of the town's security team, wanted to touch such bodies and risk suffering the vengeance of their ghosts.

Xiang-hua swept an errant hair back from her face. "I'm ready. I'll get my coat and leave immediately."

Her grandmother—her teacher and mentor—advocated compassion for the dead and their needs. At the same time, she taught her granddaughter to never fear their vengeful spirits. "Worry about the living," she would say, "not about what's beyond your control."

"I expected as much. I'll go with you," her father said, nodding resignedly. "Go, bring Xiang-hua's robe," he ordered the maid who had accompanied her into the room.

Shortly thereafter, Xiang-hua, her father, and the security team's messenger left the house and hastened through the nearly vacant streets. The day loomed heavily before her. The air, already redolent with early morning cooking fires, reminded her that she'd not yet had breakfast. Given her mission, that may have been a good thing.

As they rounded the final corner, Xiang-hua spotted a house and yard enclosed by a short mud wall. Nothing remarkable, nothing to distinguish it from the adjacent houses. A half-dozen men milled around its front courtyard. Except for Xin Fen-peng, a distantly related fellow clansman, the rest were strangers. While still early, she was sure the number of onlookers would certainly grow as the news spread about the dead man.

Zhong and the herbalist stood close together, deep in conversation. The herbalist's hands shook back and forth in front of his chest, as if in forceful denial. His face reflected a rapidly changing landscape of concern, innocence, and sincerity.

Zhong spotted the trio approaching the gate and stepped forward to meet them. The herbalist followed closely behind.

"Master Xin Chu and Sister Xiang-hua," he greeted them using the honorific often given Xiang-hua, and thereby honoring her position as a women's doctor. "I'm sorry to involve you in this matter, but it couldn't be helped." He gestured in the direction of the pigpen. "A body was discovered early this morning. The death looks suspicious. I'll have to make an official report."

As he spoke, they walked over to the pen. A large sow lay in the opposite side, suckling her piglets.

Xiang-hua studied the area. She couldn't tell much from where she stood, except that the earth just within the enclosure's gate had been churned up more than in any other area.

"Is that where the body was found?" she asked, pointing to the disturbed ground.

Zhong nodded.

"And you suspect foul play?" her father asked.

"That's right," He looked over at the man he'd sent as a messenger. "Didn't he tell you? That's why I need a coroner: to officially examine the victim," Zhong replied. "Otherwise I wouldn't have bothered you."

Chu swept his hand in front of him as if pushing something away. "Of course." He glanced briefly at Xiang-hua. "Our family is honored to be of service."

"I realize it's not easy. Thank you for coming." With that, he pointed to the western side of the courtyard where two men, wearing tattered clothing, squatted on the ground near a plank supporting the shrouded corpse. Although quite thin, they were strong. Their taut, sinewy muscles marked them as laborers; their clothing betrayed their poverty. For such men, malignant spirits weren't as risky as starvation from having no work at all.

"I had the body removed and placed over there." The rising sun produced a long patch of shadow spreading out from the house. It darkened the ominous bulky mass. "Better to keep the body in shade as long as possible."

He led them over.

The odor of damp earth hung heavily about the yard. Death's pungent stench hadn't yet permeated the air. He couldn't have been lying in the pen long.

Zhong placed a hand on top of the cloth shroud. Before removing it to expose the corpse, he warned: "The sow had already started feeding on the body by the time it was discovered."

He looked to Xiang-hua and raised his eyebrows in an unspoken question: *Was she ready?*

It was all Xiang-hua could do to control the queasiness in her stomach, but she wasn't about to let anyone see her hesitate. She was a doctor, after all. Seeing a mutilated body—while not something she'd ever experienced—shouldn't keep her from her job. Whatever that happened to be at the time. She stepped forward and nodded.

"Are you going to let a mere girl examine the man?" a voice rang out.

Startled, they turned toward the sound. It was the herbalist, Gao Shi. His glowering flushed face matched his challenge.

"She may be young, but she's a doctor just the same," Zhong replied stiffly.

"A women's doctor," Shi shot back in derision. "And she's still too young."

"I asked her to come as coroner—" Zhong started to say.

"Nonsense. What does she need to know? I've had training too. As a young man, I was an apprentice for the town's most famous bell doctor. Whatever you need, I can do it. This is too important for a child to do, much less a girl."

Xiang-hua felt her cheeks grow hot and her temper flare. Her father cleared his throat, about to speak, when Zhong hastily intervened. "Do not interfere in the work of the security team, Master Gao, or you will be reported to the court as obstructing our examination and, therefore, the court's business."

Shi blanched and stepped back. "I didn't mean to insult the security team or the court. I am simply pointing out the reality of the situation." His voice slipped into a solicitous tone. "You've seen the body. A young girl should not be subjected to that sort of thing."

Xiang-hua's eyes closed to angry slits, but her voice did not betray her annoyance. "I am quite able to handle whatever is necessary, Master Gao. You need not concern yourself."

He turned away from her and toward Zhong. "I will do whatever you say, of course. However, given the circumstances, the court may well wonder why you chose such a young person to be your coroner today. I was only trying to assist you." Shi spread his hands out before him, indicating he was giving up. Without further comment, he pivoted on his heel and slunk away.

Before Xiang-hua had time to respond, the security team leader took hold of the shroud and pulled it back.

CHAPTER 2

The students' voices rose and fell in a rhythmic cadence, giving life to the boys' Confucian lesson on how relationships form the essential foundation for both human society and heaven. The words flowed musically through the room. The sound wrapped around Shu-chang in a comforting blanket while his tapping finger matched their tempo.

Standing at the window, he gazed into the Xin courtyard with its sparsely placed pots of manicured bushes and tightly shaped trees. A small pond, embraced by a circle of rocks, claimed the area's center for itself. A tidy clump of bamboo stood in an opposite corner. Although unassuming, the garden had been carefully laid out in accordance with feng-shui rules for creating peace and prosperity.

He stared absently into the courtyard and ruminated on the students' lesson on Confucius's teaching on maintaining a peaceful country. Finally, he shifted around to his class.

"Enough," he said. The boys stopped their sing-song recitations. "Tell me what you are reading. What was Confucius asserting?"

Blank looks.

9

Shu-chang pointed to a young fellow in a corner seat. "Are the rules he's laying down complicated?"

"No, Teacher. They are simple."

"What did Confucius say to do?" he asked another who had looked up and inadvertently caught Shu-chang's eye.

He pursed his lips, then said: "Each person's duty is to live his life according to his place in society. Father, son; ruler, subject; husband, wife; elder and younger brother; friend to friend."

"Excellent. And why is it important for people to fulfill their roles?" He pointed to a bushy headed student.

"If everyone behaved correctly toward each other, the country would be at peace," he said.

Shu-chang nodded, causing the boy's lip to curve up into a satisfied grin.

"This is an important section for us to remember. Read through the text once more," Shu-chang said.

Their voices once more took up a sing-song cadence, giving Shu-chang a small surge of satisfaction. His young charges were learning something under him after all. He reached out and touched the text. *Behave according to your place in life*. Such a simple rule. Shu-chang shook his head. Then why was there so much conflict, pain, and misery? Why couldn't people just behave the way they were supposed to?

As often happened, an unbidden image of his slain father and uncle pushed into his inner vision, crowding out everything else. A marauding gang had attacked their home village and killed his father and uncle, leaving Shu-chang alone, the last of his paternal line.

His ancestral village was poor and insignificant. Why target it? Why attack it? What could the thieves and murderers gain but a few bags of rice? So far, no one knew who was behind the assault or what the attackers expected to gain. What could have been worth killing for?

Shu-chang wiped a hand over his eyes. He had been in the provincial capital at the time of their deaths, taking the second level of the national examinations. The exams. His father dreamed of Shu-chang achieving status and wealth for the family, and the exams were a critical step towards those goals. Now, Shu-chang had a second mandate: to bring justice for his father and uncle. He vowed he would find their murderers. It was his filial duty.

He looked around the clan school's only classroom and at the five young, bored faces of his charges. All the boys were related to each other through their fathers. They all belonged to the Xin clan, Shu-chang's mother's clan. When Shu-chang was left destitute and without a family, his mother's brother had turned up to support him in his loss. The school needed a teacher, and Uncle Xin offered him a lifeline: a job instructing the Xin family boys.

Truth be told, his students were not interested in struggling with the hard work of pursuing the empire's most valued measure of success: passing the three levels of examinations necessary to become a government official with all its rights and privileges. Their parents may have that wish, but even they couldn't manage the focus and commitment such a journey required. Their fathers had the best of intentions; nevertheless, many of them frequently pulled their sons out of class to help on the farm. During harvest season, every family member worked.

His gaze rested on an empty chair at the back of the room. Xiao-ren's chair. Shu-chang frowned as he gazed at the empty seat. Xiao-ren was an only son and came from a distinguished family of achievers. His paternal line was marked by distinction in governmental service, mercantile success, and medical accomplishments.

He stifled a sigh. No matter what Shu-chang did as a teacher, Xiao-ren seemed bent on squandering his advantages. He was more likely to be found running around the streets than studying and preparing for his future.

Shu-chang wiped his fingers over his eyebrow and closed his eyes. An image of a young woman with an intense, bright face filled his vision. Xiang-hua, Xiao-ren's sister. The two were his mother's cousin's children and, thus, his matrilineal cousins.

A shadow of a smile drifted over his face as he thought of Xiang-hua. She and her younger brother seemed different in every way. Although only two years older than Xiao-ren, she was already making a name for herself as a women's doctor.

Shu-chang shook his head. She exemplified everything the family wanted in their children: hard working, smart, focused. She thrived in her studies—in reading, writing, researching. All traits he admired in her. Hers was a learned, medical family—her grandfather and grandmother were both renowned doctors. Xiang-hua had studied under her grandmother's tutelage since she was a mere child—barely strong enough to use a mortar and pestle in grinding herbs. In time, simple laboratory work led to hands-on patient diagnosis and treatment. She'd quickly and ably absorbed her lessons and gained her medical training through an apprenticeship.

Her grandfather died after a good, long life. People still spoke of his medical abilities and praised his life-saving skills. And her grandmother was currently reaping the benefits of a highly successful career. Her reputation had reached the capital and the emperor's first wife. She specifically requested that Xiang-hua's grandmother come to serve as the personal physician for all of the emperor's wives and concubines. As a result, her grandmother was presently residing in the capital, leaving her granddaughter to spread her wings on her own. Now, although only at the beginning of her career, her family hoped that she would also become a notable doctor in her field. Hopes, Shu-chang was sure, she would fulfill.

He admired his maternal cousin for her intelligence and for her willingness to follow her family's guidance in her training. He frowned and shifted uncomfortably, bringing his hand over his heart. With such training and the willful stubbornness it seemed to encourage, he wondered if this path to education was proper for a young woman. Perhaps it was excessive. It wasn't his place to say anything, but he did worry about his cousin's future. She wasn't a boy, after all.

Most well-brought-up young women learned how to maintain a household. Their education didn't need to go beyond reading the Book on Filial Piety. For the more clever, he'd heard that reading and writing poetry was acceptable in order to entertain their husbands and to share with other women friends.

But Xiang-hua's intellectual curiosity and dedication went way beyond the average. Would it make her an undesirable marriage choice for possible future in-laws? What family would want a daughter-in-law who had such an upbringing, with all of the independence of thought she had been encouraged to develop?

Yes, such independence might make her an excellent doctor, but would it make her a good daughter-in-law? He shook his head. The most desirable characteristics of a daughter-in-law were obedience and unquestioning care of the family. Submission, not independence.

As the students' voices droned on, Shu-chang focused again on Xiao-ren's vacant chair. As much as he didn't want to say it, he knew the boy hated school. His need for movement overpowered his ability to focus quietly and to follow through with his studies.

Until recently, Xiao-ren had fought against his family's demands to achieve academic and professional success. Shu-chang was sure the boy wanted to make his family proud but felt inadequate when compared to his older sister. His defiance of his family's expectations of him led to his joining a nefarious faction of the rich and powerful Gao clan. That decision in turn led to his imprisonment and torture.

The young teacher rubbed the back of his neck as he recalled being instrumental in saving Xiao-ren by proving his innocence. The result was that the boy formed an exaggerated sense of loyalty and devotion to Shu-chang.

Xia-ren's loyalty meant that he now tried valiantly to be a better student and at least attend classes. Unfortunately, it didn't mean he always made it to class on time or did his required assignments. Shu-chang sighed and shook his head. Xiao-ren probably overslept. Again.

Being a teacher gave Shu-chang a livelihood and a roof over his head, but it had proved to be a double edge sword in his pursuit of justice for his family. It delayed him because, as a teacher, he had daily, full-time duties that ate up his time. However, it also allowed him to pursue his quest for retribution for his father and uncle's murders by gathering information about the goings-on in the region in his spare time. As the largest market town in the area, it was the center of a network of people and communication. Everyone and everything eventually passed through here. He was sure that through persistence he would find the gang that murdered his family. Even if it took a lifetime.

As he stared out the window lost in thought, the thumping of running feet on the wooden veranda caught his attention. Shu-chang turned just as Xiao-ren burst into the room.

"Xiao-ren, don't run! You're late," Shu-chang barked. The other boys immediately stopped their singsong chanting. Their attention transferred completely to the irascible Xiao-ren and his new antics. Shu-chang whirled around, facing his class. "Continue with your reading."

All heads immediately bent over their books in apparent

submission while surreptitiously keeping watch on their teacher and Xiao-ren.

Seeing that Xiao-ren remained at the doorway, still trying to recover his breath, Shu-chang ordered: "Xiao-ren, sit down. You're already in trouble, don't make it worse." He strode over to his desk and glared at the boy.

Shu-chang, as the clan school's teacher, tried to take a strict stance toward his charges. It wasn't easy for him, but he felt it was expected and necessary. The clan's consensus was that young people wouldn't respect authority if shown leniency in their tasks. And respect was the cornerstone of proper, acceptable behavior. And of a moral society.

He did his best, although at times he permitted more leeway than their parents would approve of. His habit of occasionally allowing the boys to speak casually to him or talk among themselves could be a source of tension between him and the Xin clan leaders—if they knew of it. They would certainly assert that Xiao-ren's poor behavior was due to Shu-chang's lack of strictness.

Xiao-ren, breathing heavily, bent over with his hands on his knees. Beads of sweat trickled down his forehead. Finally, he inhaled long and deep, let his breath out, straightened up, and entered the classroom, halting in front of Shu-chang's table.

"I don't want excuses. Sit down and stop making a spectacle," Shu-chang said, pointing to the empty chair in the back of the room. It was not uncommon for his student to come dashing into class either just in time or late. Shu-chang couldn't let the other students think that such behavior was acceptable. No telling where it would end.

"I ... There's—" Xiao-ren gasped between gulps of air. Strands of his ink-black hair plastered against his cheeks went unnoticed.

Shu-chang couldn't hold back his concern any longer. He

moved toward him and put his hand on Xiao-ren's shoulder, to calm him. "What happened? What's going on?"

The boy took a couple more deep breaths to steady himself and looked up at his teacher with big, round eyes. "They found a body in Gao Shi's pigpen!"

CHAPTER 3

The classroom broke out into a cacophony of gasps and exclamations. Gao Shi, a well-known local herbalist, lived alone in a modest farmhouse not too far from the classroom. Most families had used his potions, tinctures, and herbs at one time or another. He grew many of his medicinal plants himself and, as with many people, he also raised a few chickens and pigs. A small area of his courtyard had been walled off for a sow and her piglets.

"Are you sure? How did you find out?"

"People are already talking about it on the streets. I ran into a farmer who was going to his fields and had just passed Gao's place. Apparently, there's already quite a gathering of spectators."

Xiao-ren's inadvertent admission that he was out on the streets when he should have been in class was not lost on Shu-chang. He resolved to talk to his young cousin about that later.

"Has the village security team's leader been notified?" Shu-chang asked instead of reprimanding him.

Still breathing heavily, Xiao-ren managed: "Yes. They

found Gao Zhong working in his field. He immediately called the members of the security team together. They've already arrived."

"What did Zhong decide about the death?" Shu-chang asked. All unusual deaths had to be investigated to determine if they were natural or not. Because the provincial magistrate lived some distance away in the area's largest city, Zhong—as the village security leader—was responsible for gathering all of the appropriate information in the case.

Xiao-ren, now recovered from his exertion, straightened to his full height. "Zhong believes the death was suspicious, so he needs the advice of a coroner." His voice resonated with the serious implications of Zhong's conclusion.

Shu-chang nodded. According to the law, a suspicious death required a thorough investigation, and that usually required the aid of a coroner.

Xiao-ren went on: "The old woman who usually confirms the cause of death is out of town." He paused and flashed a proud grin. "Zhong needed someone to fill in for the coroner. He sent a messenger to the house to get Xiang-hua."

"Xiang-hua!" Shu-chang cringed at the thought of her having to see the body. "Why Xiang-hua? She's too young for that sort of thing." Even though he knew it was common for women to be coroners, they were older women. Much older. Married or widowed. They had already experienced much as mid-wives. Not young, unmarried women. That was wrong. The idea repulsed him.

Xiao-ren barely lifted his shoulders in reply. "She's a doctor. No one else is available. She's the best trained medical person in town. Much more qualified than the old lady who normally does the job for Zhong," he added as a simple statement of fact.

Shu-chang looked out across the courtyard toward a door on the far side leading to Xiang-hua's family's residence.

Years ago, her grandfather's two sons had divided the compound into separate residential areas. Today, their descendants—Uncle Xin and Master Chu—still lived in their respective branches of the family home. They shared the courtyard and wandered freely back and forth between residences. It proved to be a happy arrangement on all sides.

Such living quarters also meant that Shu-chang, who lived with his Uncle Xin, found himself residing in the same compound with Xiang-hua and Xiao-ren, although in a different residence. As a result, he knew Xiang-hua quite well. They had worked together in the past to solve her brother's crippling brush with the law. He recalled her determined dark eyes sparkling with curiosity, excited at every new discovery, and the way she tucked her head down when she worked out something she didn't quite understand.

He pushed his hands into his sleeves. Certainly, he admitted to himself, her intelligence and work ethic captured his respect. How could they not?

He clasped his hands behind his back and lifted his chin. He ruminated briefly once more, however, on her following in her grandmother's footsteps as a women's doctor. It wasn't a proper calling for a young, unmarried woman from a good home. Female doctors ran all over town visiting patients with who-knows-what kind of illnesses. They went alone. Unsupervised.

Such freedom worried him. What would it lead to? It would be better for Xiang-hua to stay safely at home reading, learning, and writing poetry that she could share with her like-minded friends. If she had them. Or, better yet, doing embroidery and learning how to run an efficient household. Preparing to be a good daughter-in-law and wife. Not this. Not a women's doctor. No matter what good she thought she did for the women.

There were plenty of bell doctors, those trained through

various types of apprenticeships, and other well-trained, educated doctors. Her skills weren't essential, he mused frowning. Others could do that work, he was sure. Why her?

As if sensing his displeasure, Xiao-ren said in defense of his sister: "She had to go. The security leader sent for her. It's her duty."

Finally, Shu-chang nodded. "Yes. She had no choice." He exhaled forcefully before adding, "I hope the body wasn't in the pen for long."

The other boys' eyes grew large. They understood what he meant. Pigs would eat meat found in their pens, whatever the source, and a nursing sow would certainly attack such a find with gusto.

To distance himself from the image and the troublesome subject of Xiang-hua's involvement, Shu-chang asked, "When the messenger came to the house, did he say who found the body?"

"A peddler passed by the pen early this morning on his way to market. Apparently, he's fond of Shi's pig and often stops to scratch her head. But not this morning she didn't come when he called to her. He heard her grunting and when he looked for her, he saw the pig standing over something large. A man lying on the ground." Xiao-ren paused and took several deep breaths, the only sound in the silence that followed. It was as if the students all held their breath not wanting to lose a single detail.

"What did he do next?" Shu-chang prodded. "Did he talk to the herbalist or go to the town's security team immediately?"

"From what the messenger told father, he went to the security team's leader Mister Gao Zhong. When he arrived at the house, Zhong was already gone. After explaining the situation to his wife, she told him he could find her husband out in the fields. Fortunately, his farmland is nearby."

Shu-chang nodded. "Yes. He was right to go to Zhong first. The security team should always be notified straight away." He pursed his lips in thought. "However, it seems to me that the peddler would want to find out if the man were truly dead or how bad his injuries were. Or at least notify Shi about the man, so that Shi could check on him."

"I heard that because it was early, a few people were on the road going to their fields. The peddler had one of them alert Shi. But he also told them not to go into the pen until Zhong arrived. I guess the peddler already believed the guy was dead."

"Smart fellow," Shu-chang said. "And, from what you know, was everything left in place, undisturbed, by the time Zhong got to the scene?"

Xiao-ren's eyes slid to the side, as he tried to remember what he'd heard. "After the security chief heard what the peddler saw, he gathered his team together. In no time, they arrived at Shi's house. The body hadn't been moved. It was still in the pen. Although by then the herbalist had confined the pig," Xiao-ren added almost as an afterthought.

The boys crossed their arms over their chests, as if to protect themselves from the horror they were hearing about. Their movement drew Shu-chang's attention and reminded him of his responsibilities as their teacher.

He looked out over his charges. "The village will take care of this tragedy. You heard Xiao-ren; the security team is already at the site. You don't need to worry." He glanced back at Xiao-ren, whose eyes still shone with excitement. "You can take your seat now. I'm sure we'll all find out what happened later."

The young man nodded, pushed back his shoulders, and marched to the back of the room, head high, a smug smile tugging at his lips. The other students all gaped at him.

Keeping the students on task proved to be even more

challenging than usual after Xiao-ren's revelation. Their recitation of the Confucian text wavered. While Xiao-ren had taken his place at the table and ostensibly mouthed the material, the rest of the class could not so easily camouflage their distractions. The death demanded their full attention. They wanted to wallow in every lurid detail Xiao-ren could offer, even if he had to improvise. Confucius didn't stand a chance.

After an agonizingly interminable long period of work, it was finally time for lunch. Shu-chang released the boys after giving them a short memorization assignment for tomorrow's class. Although emanating tension with every step, the students filed out of the classroom and through the Xin courtyard as noiselessly as possible. As soon as they were out the gate, however, their boisterous discussions erupted. Their voices surged back to the classroom. Shu-chang had no doubt they would all manage to go past herbalist Shi's pigsty on the way to their homes.

Xiao-ren remained. "Will you be going over?" he asked.

"No. As I said, it's a legal matter and the security team will take care of it." Shu-chang closed his book and put his desk in order.

The young man rose and slowly approached the front. Before reaching Shu-chang's desk, he paused. Watching his teacher, a sharp line cut between his eyes, giving him a troubled expression. "Aren't you even interested? What if it's murder? You could investigate."

Hearing his questions, Shu-chang almost grinned. His young cousin viewed him as a sort of avenger for justice, a fanciful belief Shu-chang attributed to his exuberant youthfulness. And he had no doubt that Xiao-ren would want to be his side-kick in the investigation.

"What?" Shu-chang asked, attempting to maintain a show of disinterest. "This is not my business."

Xiao-ren's eyes reflected his disappointment. He glanced at the ground. "What can Zhong do if it's a murder? He's just a farmer. He can barely read and write. The only reason he was appointed the security team's leader is because he's one of the Gao clan elders."

"Don't be so disrespectful," Shu-chang admonished. "He's smarter than you think. He just didn't have the opportunity to go to school. You'd be better off if you were as clever as that farmer."

Xiao-ren shuffled his feet and looked down. "I apologize," he said, although he couldn't help adding: "But, you know what I mean."

Shu-chang sighed. Shaking his head, he rubbed his chin. "None of this is up to me. I can't interfere with the security team. Plus, if the death does turn out to be suspicious, it will become the court's business and the magistrate will do a thorough investigation."

Shoulders slumped, Xiao-ren continued to stare at the hard-packed dirt floor.

"All right," Shu-chang relented. "I'll talk to your sister. With her acting as coroner in this case, I should be able to learn more and find out what's really going on."

"Great!" The boy's eyes lit up.

"I didn't say I'd investigate, just that I'll look into the case," Shu-chang said. He shoved his hands in the opposite sleeves of his robe, crossing his chest. "Satisfied?"

Xiao-ren nodded quickly, beamed, and ran out the door.

Shu-chang watched him go and shook his head. Xiao-ren was a complex mixture of youthful naïveté with insight beyond his years.

Turning back to his table, he began to gather up his materials and, with some trepidation, wonder what he was getting himself into.

CHAPTER 4

"**P**repare yourself. It's not a pretty sight," Zhong murmured.

As he removed the shroud, Xiang-hua steeled herself and slipped closer to the body. Her father shadowed her every move. His presence was both a comfort and a reminder of her vulnerabilities. She would not let him down. His allowing her to answer Zhong's request proved he had confidence in her and her skills.

Bending over the body, she began her examination.

The sow had not yet made significant progress in her meal, but that made the mud-covered corpse no less horrific. She had torn off the man's left ear, and only half of his shredded face remained.

A wave of nausea swept over Xiang-hua. Her stomach lurched and she clasped a hand firmly over her mouth as she began to totter. A hand grabbed her, steadying her. She briefly turned away from the corpse and looked up. Her father held tightly to her arm. His stricken eyes bore into hers, and his sickly pallor betrayed his own revulsion at the sight before them. He looked like he was about to faint himself. Nevertheless, he firmly held onto her, providing support.

She braced herself once more and took a couple of long, deep breaths. Thankful that the stench of death had not yet reached out its putrid talons, she relaxed. A bit. With a nod to her father, she returned to the mutilated corpse.

"I'm sorry," Zhong said to her father. "Perhaps Shi was right. I shouldn't have asked your daughter to be our coroner today."

Mortified by her weakness, Xiang-hua quickly said, "I'm a trained doctor, and you needed someone."

Zhong exhaled noisily. "Of course. But perhaps I should have gone to one of the old women in town. Another midwife. The law accepts anyone with some medical experience. I could have even asked a bell doctor," Zhong said.

"Yes," her father said in a shaking voice. "Almost anyone with any medical training would do." He obviously hadn't realized the enormity of the situation when he'd permitted his daughter to participate in this gruesome task.

Xiang-hua heard the regret in his voice. With determination, she focused on the corpse. Her gaze swept over the entire body before she knelt at its side.

Her father started to reach for her arm again but then pulled back and remained standing behind her without interfering.

Relieved to see that the sow hadn't had time to start on other body parts, she proceeded. The victim, who was built much the same as the men Zhong had hired to move him, wore a short, rough, cotton jacket and pants tied below the knees. His cloth hat clung in a macabre fashion to his head; a beleaguered, muddied white feather limply hung in its turned-up rim. Avoiding the head at first, she began a careful analysis by scrutinizing each hand and the exposed chest. The hands revealed a man used to a hard life of heavy work: dirty, broken fingernails and calluses on his fingers. Hardened calluses also covered the bottoms of his bare feet. Otherwise, neither his hands nor feet showed signs of trauma.

Xiang-hua opened the man's jacket to examine his whole upper body. As she did, a folded piece of paper slipped out. She glanced up at Zhong, who raised his eyebrows but remained silent. She unfolded the paper, forming a long, cream-colored slip. Characters written with black ink covered the front. Taoist symbols were stamped on the opposite side. Holding the paper up, she tried to read the characters. No luck. They were indecipherable.

She passed the note to Zhong, who held it this way and that, squinting until his face resembled a shriveled apple.

"This writing doesn't make sense. It looks like characters," Zhong said, handing the paper to her father.

Grasping it by the tips of his fingers, he studied the writing without comment. Finally, passing the slip back to Zhong, he said with certainty: "These are not normal characters."

Xiang-hua nodded. "I agree. I'd guess this is ghost writing. Supernatural writing."

"If that's the case, who can we get to read it for us?" Zhong asked.

"A shaman might be able to translate what it means. Or maybe only the medium who wrote this in the first place," Xiang-hua said.

"That means we need to talk to a Taoist," her father said with a frown.

Xiang-hua shifted her weight and sat back on her heels. "It's probably some kind of protective charm. We can ask the Taoist priest, Master Yan-du, to decipher the writings." She stared down at the corpse. "This man must have been worried about something to seek out a protective charm like this."

Zhong looked over at one of his men. "Go get Master Yan-du and bring him here straight away." He hit a fist into his open hand. "Maybe he can identify the victim and help us bring an end to the case. The sooner I can send an account to the court, the happier I'll be."

Xiang-hua returned to her task. She'd inspected the hands, feet, and upper body; it was time to move on. Mentally hardening herself, she proceeded to the victim's head and neck. He stared up at her, his one eye wide open, bone shinning through where the other eye would have been. She leaned closer and, as she did, she heard her father catch his breath. She forced herself to look closely into his eye and saw unusual, tiny, red spots. Gently rotating his head from side to side, she studied him. No trauma outside of the disfigurement caused by the sow.

"Did the sow kill him?" Zhong asked, throwing a baleful look at the pig who lay corralled in the far corner with her nursing piglets.

"That could be a reasonable deduction, since he is in the pen," Shi said. Xiang-hua glanced over at him in surprise. She hadn't noticed him return to their small group. He continued assertively, "The man was probably a thief, trying to steal my sow. His bad luck that he tripped and fell, startling the pig. She reacted by attacking and killing him. Sows can be quite dangerous when they're lactating. They have fearsome appetites and piglets to protect."

"Anything is possible," Zhong said. "What do you say, Xiang-hua?"

"It's too early to tell." She motioned toward the corpse. "He needs to be turned over."

"Whatever for?" Shi grimaced.

As one, the gawkers' muttering rose in obvious repulsion at the request.

"I'm not finished with my examination," Xiang-hua said simply.

No one approached. No one wanted to touch the body—not even the beggars Zhong had commandeered to remove it from the pen. The little bit he promised to pay them didn't make them willing to do more than they had already.

"Shi is right," Zhong said. "We've seen enough. You can write this up, as is, in the report."

Xiang-hua shook her head. Her job wasn't complete. With difficulty, she grasped the body and turned it over, revealing a jagged cut in the lower back, at the center of a large, dark stain on his jacket. The men around her gasped.

She ignored the crowd's confused comments. Dredging up what she'd read in her grandfather's book about how to gather forensic information, Xiang-hua sifted through her medicine bag. She quickly removed a small measuring stick. After a momentary glance toward the cowering laborers, she asked Zhong to push the jacket up while she measured the cut's length and width.

He barked an order to a couple of the hired men to remove the coat and stepped aside.

Again, bending close to the body, she peered at the wound. It was deep. Meticulously assessing its size, Xiang-hua read the dimensions to the security chief.

But that wasn't the only thing. A tattoo wrapped around his upper left arm. Whether gods or demons, she couldn't be sure. She glanced at Zhong and caught his attention. He nodded, seeming to read her thoughts. Tattoos were rare. From what she'd heard, criminals sometimes had tattoos. They were a charm, giving them protection in their dangerous profession. It was a source of defense against the perceived evil around them. Nevertheless, even among thieves it was uncommon. Permanently altering one's body desecrated it, an extremely disrespectful and unfilial act.

Parents gave children their bodies, and their gift was never to be defiled. Xiang-hua had only heard of gang members being willing to break this expectation.

She shot a quick glance at Shi. What was this man doing here in the herbalist's pen? Was Shi mixed up in some criminal activity?

She shook her head, reminding herself to stay on task. It wasn't her job to cast suspicion on anyone. She was here to perform a medical duty only. "I will write up my findings for you, Master Zhong, to include in your report to the magistrate," she said. "I believe it was the stab wound that killed him, not the pig. He was probably dead before being thrown into the pen."

Zhong cast a sour look at the herbalist.

"What! Impossible! Who would do such a thing? And why is he here?" Shi's voice rose an octave. His eyes bored through Xiang-hua. "You're mistaken." He swung around to the security team's leader. "I told you she was too young to do this. Too silly. Too dramatic. How can you trust a child with such a conclusion? If you report this as a murder, you'll not only be a laughing stock, you'll create a big problem for yourself and for the town. The emperor will not be happy with such a capricious judgement."

Zhong rubbed his chin. "How do you explain the knife wound, if not for murder?"

"He could have gotten in a fight and been stabbed. He looks like a rough type of guy. After being hurt, he tried to leave, took some wrong turns, ended up in my pigpen. What else could have happened?" Shi said defiantly, his voice tight with anger.

"That's still murder!" Zhong said.

"Look at him. I'll bet you anything no one will claim to know him, much less care that he died. Do you honestly think the magistrate wants to be bothered with this?" Shi sneered and waved a dismissive hand over the corpse. "You'd do better to just take him out and bury him the way the city buries its homeless who die on the streets. There's no need for a report."

Zhong pursed his lips and looked at the young doctor. "Are you sure Xiang-hua?" Ringing his hands, he added, "This case can cause all kinds of trouble for our town if you're wrong."

The security chief's growing indecision was painful. Catching her father about to defend her, however, she quickly responded: "I would not deceive you, Sir. As I said, I will write up my observations and conclusions. If I don't give the true facts, this man's ghost will never forgive us. More deaths may follow." The victim was poor, and perhaps even a thug, but that didn't merit such a death. He still deserved justice.

Xiang-hua knew that her youth was a strike against her in this case, but Zhong had asked her to come. She had to do her best as an honest coroner. Then, too, she admitted to herself that she didn't want the town to think she could be easily swayed in her medical opinions. That could have serious consequences down the road. Young or not, she had to stand firm.

"Really, Zhong," Shi interrupted. "When Granny Ao-po is your coroner, she doesn't decide for you whether a person died from natural causes or not, she merely tells you what she observes about the body. Why are you letting this pullet tell you what's what?"

Xiang-hua wanted to speak out but remained silent. Nevertheless, her brain reeled and her heart burned in anger.

"Zhong, you asked her to come because you trusted her expertise and training," Xiang-hua's father said. "Granny Ao-po is a good woman, but she doesn't have Xiang-hua's level of knowledge. She's not a formally trained doctor. You have a day or two before you need to send a report to the magistrate. Why don't you investigate further, then decide what to do? Of course, you'll have the full cooperation of my family in this."

Zhong looked at the corpse and then Xiang-hua. "You've shown great strength in performing the duties of a coroner. The least I can do is my job as the city's security chief." He turned to Shi, "We will be investigating this death further."

"I'll send a report on the condition of the body to you later today," Xiang-hua said.

CHAPTER 5

Shu-chang hung his brush up on its holder, allowing its bristles to maintain their shape. Xiao-ren's news excited him. He glanced out into the courtyard, wondering if Xiang-hua had returned. He was impatient to find out what she'd discovered. *Certainly not to get involved. Just out of general curiosity,* he avowed to himself. He caught sight of a passing maid and inquired about Xiang-hua and her father. No, they were not back yet.

He continued to busy himself with putting the classroom in order while his mind danced around this intriguing new development. And Xiang-hua's role in it. He was impatient to see her. He wanted to learn more about the death and he also wondered how she was doing. He frowned as he thought of his young cousin having to contend with a murder victim.

By the time he'd completed the day's cleanup, Shu-chang had decided to go to the herbalist's. A number of the locals were probably there already, anyway. He was only being inquisitive about an unusual event. A normal reaction, he told himself as he grabbed his robe. Before he could leave, however, Uncle Xin's wife, Aunt Nu-er, popped in. An unpretentious woman, she was the cornerstone of Uncle Xin's life. A plethora of tiny grease spots covered her dusky-blue, mid-length tunic. Errant strands of long black hair fanned out around her head. Nevertheless, her plump cheeks and sparkling eyes gave her a decidedly welcoming appearance.

"I've prepared lunch. Come and eat. Your Uncle Xin is home, you can join him."

"I'll be right there," Shu-chang enthusiastically agreed. Although only of medium build, he never turned down an invitation to a meal. He grinned in expectation. Aunt Nu-er was an excellent cook.

"He's in the main room," she said over her shoulder as she bustled out the door. "Food's already on the table. Don't make him wait for you."

Shu-chang nodded. "I'm going. I'll be there before you," he kidded.

"Humph. Not likely," she said, but he could see her lips pull up into a smile.

Being childless and of modest means, Uncle Xin never felt it necessary to develop a women's quarter in his wing of the U-shaped compound he shared with his cousin Chu. Thus, his wife moved freely throughout the entire house. Chu, in contrast, had built separate women's quarters. Nevertheless, from what Shu-chang could tell, that didn't keep Xiang-hua restricted in any way.

The smells of spices and onion greeted him as he approached Uncle Xin's study. He inhaled their promise, and his stomach rumbled in anticipation.

As he stepped over the threshold, his uncle called out, "Glad you could join me. Big news about today."

Shu-chang nodded and sat on a heavy wooden stool at a small game table. Several dishes of food crowded together on a serving tray along with a couple of empty bowls. As he settled down, Aunt Nu-er entered the room and placed a covered porcelain container between them. She removed the lid, revealing a steaming bowl of rice. The men each scooped a healthy portion of the white grain into their bowls.

Shu-chang, using the back of his chopsticks, reached out toward the shredded chicken. He placed several slim pieces of it on his uncle's rice, then took a few for himself. Before shoveling the chicken and rice into his mouth, however, he paused. Looking up at his uncle, he said: "Xiao-ren came to the classroom earlier. He said a man was found in the herbalist's pigsty."

"It looks bad. Foul play for sure." Uncle Xin glanced aside, then at his bowl. "Did he tell you his sister was the coroner?"

Shu-chang slowly nodded his head in agreement. Uncle Xin didn't look any happier about the situation than he was.

"The security team leader asked her to come. Wish he hadn't. Yes, she's a doctor, but she's only seventeen. It would be different if he'd asked her grandmother. Although, even then, I would have been surprised. Grandmother Xin is learned and famous for her skills. Too famous to do the work of a coroner." When he said the last word, his tone did nothing to mask his low opinion of the job. He jabbed at the chicken. "I suppose her father had to let her go. How could they refuse? Still—"

"Mm-mm," Shu-chang murmured. He completely agreed with the unspoken criticism, but it wasn't his place to fault her father's decision. He ducked his head to hide any disagreements his face might betray. His chopsticks hovered over a bowl of thinly sliced, mixed pickled vegetables as if he were deciding on which piece to add to his dish.

"She's had excellent training," Uncle Xin immediately added, as if to deny the implied disapproval of his cousin.

"That's not the issue. The security chief should have found someone else. The coroner's job isn't complicated. If the person has an obvious wound, call it a suspicious death. If not, don't. It doesn't take a highly trained doctor." He finished, clamping his mouth shut into a tight line.

Uncle Xin jabbed his chopsticks into a dish of stir-fried vegetables mixed with sesame sauce. "You've noticed her father didn't go into medicine; he sees being a merchant as much less troublesome all the way around."

"She appears to be passionate about her work. She thinks she's helping other women when they most need it," Shu-chang said in Xiang-hua's defense.

Uncle Xin sighed. "Yes, that and fulfilling her grandparents' expectations. If she hadn't become a doctor, there would be no one to carry on their medical tradition. The next step is for her to marry another doctor and join the two medical families. That way the family's unique knowledge won't be lost. It'll still be held securely within the family—the extended family."

Shu-chang cringed but nodded. The Xin name was renowned within the medical community. Over the generations, they had developed various idiosyncratic but highly effective medicines and techniques. These would never be taught to outsiders, and lived on only through their family's practice. Most medical families held tightly to their curative discoveries. The basis of medicine and medical techniques were written in books and taught to the best male students at the national university. The most successful families, however, built their reputations by refining this vast store of knowledge through experience. These improvements were valuable and closely held secrets.

Shu-chang wondered whether Chu would really commit his only daughter in marriage to another family and husband based solely on the family's profession. Would he do that to make up for his avoiding the medical profession himself, as a way of compensating and fulfilling his own failed duty to his parents? And then he thought of Xiang-hua. Would she, could she, challenge her family and not accept such a marriage?

He scowled and turned aside from the question. It really wasn't his business. But then, he argued with himself, she was like a sister to him. That's why he worried about her and her future. A sister. He shifted uncomfortably in his chair because he knew he was deceiving himself. She was not a sister or related to him through his father's lineage. She was his mother's brother's daughter, and in traditional families that would make her his perfect spouse. Embarrassed at this line of thinking, Shu-chang cleared his throat and announced, "I'm going over to the Shi residence. If you're not busy, would you like to go along? Apparently, Xiang-hua and her father haven't come home yet."

Uncle Xin thrust his chopsticks into the air. "Excellent. Let's leave as soon as we've finished eating."

Shu-chang proceeded to dig into the many small dishes set around the table, piling tidbits from one or the other onto his rice and scooping it into his mouth.

Uncle Xin laughed. "You're a grown man but you still eat like a starving teenager."

Embarrassed, he slowed down and tried to eat with more decorum, although his stomach complained.

In time, they washed the food down with a quick cup of tea and strode from the room.

The herbalist's house was only a few blocks away. They moved swiftly through the town's narrow streets. There were few people out-and-about at midday. This was a time to enjoy a short nap, thus leaving the streets quiet.

A wiry vendor trudged toward them, his food cart filling

the narrow road. He wore the typical worker's outfit of a short jacket, pants tied at the knee, sandals made of straw, and a cloth tied around his head. Apparently, having sold his savory snacks during the early morning market, he was returning home.

Shu-chang often bought a quick lunch from him when he came to town.

"Finished already?" the young teacher called out.

Startled, the man stumbled to a stop. He stared at them as if coming out of a dream. Then, recognizing Shu-chang, he nodded. "Teacher," the man greeted him. "Yes. A short selling day. Now I'm home to work my field." He squinted at Shu-chang. The gauntness of his face accented the creases slashed across his forehead and down the sides of his mouth.

"Are you well?" Shu-chang asked. "You're looking pale."

The peddler attempted a small smile. "I'm as well as can be. This morning on my way to market, I passed the herbalist's home and found a man in his pigsty."

"Ah, you discovered the body," Uncle Xin said, unconsciously stepping away from him.

"My bad fate."

"Did you know him? Is he from the town?" Shu-chang asked.

The peddler shook his head. "No. Or, I don't know. I couldn't recognize him. He was in the pen." He stopped and looked away.

"Of course, probably covered in mud," Uncle Xin offered.

The peddler bent his head and spoke to his cart. "He was. Covered in mud. But that wasn't it. The sow had ... His face was already ..." He stammered, the sheen of sweat on his brow betraying his emotions. Finally, he blurted out: "It shredded his face!" He wiped at his forehead. "I wanted to vomit."

Shu-chang involuntarily covered his cheek with a hand. Uncle Xin closed his eyes against the image.

"Was anyone else about at that time?" Shu-chang asked.

"Too early. Although I did see Shi's neighbor, Yao-sheng, step out of his house. He placed a dish on his doorstep and immediately went back inside."

"Did he see you? Say anything?"

"No. He never looked up. He just set the dish down and went back into the house."

"Before you left Shi's, did you learn anything about what Zhong had discovered? Anything of note?" Shu-chang asked.

The peddler glanced behind him, back down the road toward Shi's house. "I don't know. I reported the body but didn't stay. I had to sell my food. It was unfortunate for the stranger, but I still have to work. I don't know anything else," he repeated as he shifted from one foot to the other.

Shu-chang tightened his lips as he regarded the peddler. How could he think of money at such a time?

The peddler again wiped at his sweaty face with his shirt sleeve, leaving a streak of dirt.

His movement reminded Shu-chang of his own father. He used to wipe away at the sweat on his face with his shirt sleeve, too. He instantly regretted his judging the peddler so harshly. His glance fell to the man's patched trousers. A peasant's life wasn't easy. Personal emotions had to be put aside in order to survive.

"Yes, of course," Shu-chang said, breaking out of his brief reverie.

"We won't keep you any longer from your work," Uncle Xin added.

Both men stepped closer to the wall, thereby clearing the narrow pathway. Once the peddler passed with his cart, they continued down the road.

Well before they could see the house, the low mumbling

of men's voices announced their destination. Rounding the corner, they saw a half dozen male and a couple of female merchants clustered near a short wall, blocking the narrow street.

They had arrived.

CHAPTER 6

F inished with her job as coroner, yet still interested in this strange case, Xiang-hua waited with her father while Zhong and his men searched the immediate area around the spot the body was first discovered. This exploration produced nothing unusual. The sow and her band of piglets had churned the mud into a homogenous mess, leaving no indication of how the dead man got into the pen.

"Given those wounds, the victim could have been killed elsewhere and dumped here," Zhong said, stopping near them. "Probably carried through the gate or tossed over the wall. It's pretty short. Keeps the pigs in, but no real barrier to a human. Of course," he cast a quick glance around, "he could also have been killed here, inside the pen. With the pigs having rooted around, we'll never find any signs of a struggle." He put his hands on his hips and glared at the trampled ground, as if he could force a confession from it. "But that begs the question of why he was here."

Zhong loudly expelled his breath and stomped away, calling out orders to his men.

Chu leaned against the wall, avoiding the sun. "Let's wait a bit before returning to the house,

Xiang-hua glanced over at him.

"To see if Zhong turns anything up," he said, watching the security chief.

Xiang-hua wanted to know more too, so she readily agreed. She moved out of the shade. *No sense in doing nothing,* she thought and approached the enclosure. She skirted the periphery of the pen, carefully examining the wall and the bare ground surrounding it. As with most such yards, only a few, annoying blades of grass managed to invade the space. All vegetation, except pots of plants or perhaps a patch of bamboo, was typically eradicated in an effort to keep out snakes and poisonous insects. Shi had banished even these bits of controlled growth, keeping the earth as bare as possible throughout the pen and the surrounding area.

Her efforts were rewarded when a torn piece of coarse, blue material caught her eye. The tattered cloth was stuck on an edge of the hardened mud wall and near the area the victim was found. Encouraged by the discovery, she continued her search. She was rewarded by finding a patch of golden seeds between the road and the shallow dirt strip surrounding the pigsty. The seeds formed a thin, short line leading toward the pen. Probably nothing. Nevertheless, she scooped them up, wrapped them in the piece of cloth, and dropped the bundle into her sleeve. Doubling her efforts at searching the area, she continued around the pen's periphery. She moved along at a slow, steady gait, eyes focused on the nearby ground and the pen's wall.

After searching both the inside and outside of the wall, she straightened and looked around for Zhong; she needed to let him know about her finds. She spotted him up at the gate talking to his men. As she was about to join him, she heard, "Xiang-hua!"

Her father was gesturing and pointing toward a man moving quickly through the road, rapidly closing the distance between himself and Zhong. The newcomer's short jacket hung askew, flapping around him, revealing an ample belly. Yan-du, the Taoist.

Zhong also recognized the priest and met him at the gate.

"Your man said you needed me. I came immediately," Yan-du called out to the security team leader.

"I heard there's been a death," he continued as he entered the tiny yard.

"Yes. Very possibly a murder," Zhong said.

"What can I do? Murder is a matter for the courts," Yan-du said, raising a hand to wipe beads of perspiration off his face. He glanced at the covered form. "Do you need an exorcism?"

"No. At least, not yet," Zhong said. "You can talk to Shi later about that."

Yan-du grunted an affirmative. "So, why am I here?"

"We've found something we need to ask you about," Zhong said. His face expressed his confusion as he drew out the folded paper found on the man's body. He paused, gripping the paper near his chest. He turned it over in his fingers, then handed it to the priest. "Can you tell me about this note?"

Xiang-hua and her father had both stepped closer, quietly listening.

Taking the paper, Yan-du unfolded and smoothed it out. Turning the paper back and forth, he studied its contents. They all remained quiet as he concentrated.

Finally, with a furrowed brow, Yan-du began: "This side," he pointed to a vertical line of forms, "indicates it's a Taoist talisman. See? You can tell by the symbols." He held the strip up, pinched between his thumb and forefinger, for them to see. With his other hand, he traced a circular form split in half by a wavy line. One section was covered in red ink, the other was plain, and each section had a dot in it.

Zhong leaned closer to get a better look and nodded. Xiang-hua waited. As with most people, she had seen Taoist talismans before. It was not uncommon to find Yan-du and other Taoist priests at tables set up in the street where they prepared and sold talismans to customers. While not everyone believed in the powers of such talismans, few people would refuse the promise of assistance. Often a charm was the first line of defense in an unsettled world. The next step, if a person had special difficulties or if he felt he needed a boost of spiritual help, would be to request an exorcism of his home or other more extreme measures.

Yan-du turned the paper over. "Now, this side is more problematic. These characters are from the supernatural world. While a medium is in a trance, a communication door opens, and he becomes a tool for the gods to write a message to the living. The characters are not of this world. They're indecipherable. Only the medium who wrote it would be able to read the ghostly writings, and, unfortunately, that wasn't me. Therefore, I'm sorry to say, I can't read this."

Disappointed, Zhong moved to retrieve the paper. As the Taoist handed it over to the security team leader, he added, "Nevertheless, I am somewhat familiar with the styles of our local priests."

A look of cautious encouragement crossed Zhong's face as he refolded and tucked the talisman into his sleeve. "Who do you think wrote this?"

"You might want to look for the Taoist with a table in front of the City God's temple. I don't know him well, but he's a regular. I believe he's there every day." Yan-du studied the charm once more, before adding, "His specialty is the protective amulet. Many, many people come to him. Very likely this is his. He might be able to tell you more about the man."

Zhong nodded. "Come," he said. "There's more." He led Yan-du over to the corpse. Xiang-hua, keeping her distance, quietly followed behind them. Zhong pulled the shirt back, revealing the tattoo on the man's shoulder. "Do you recognize this?"

Yan-du stepped closer to the body and bent down for a closer look. After gazing at the tattoo for a time, he stood up and faced Zhong. "They're demons with Taoist symbols," he said tersely in a muted voice. "Everyone knows that. They're not unusual."

"But not as a tattoo," Zhong said. "That's not common, is it?"

"Tattoos themselves are uncommon. Who knows what the unscrupulous will do—even with sacred symbols?" Yan-du spread out his hands to reinforce his words. "I don't know if this is the tattoo, but I have heard of a gang that tattoos its members once they've been fully initiated into the group."

Zhong's eyebrows danced in pleasure. "If we can find other similar tattoos, we might get somewhere on this case."

"Do you think there's any relationship between the tattoo and his talisman?" Xiang-hua asked.

Yan-du started and turned to the young doctor. "Ah, Sister, I didn't notice you when I first arrived." He looked around at the scene. "I'm sorry we're meeting under such unhappy circumstances." He gave her a grave smile.

She nodded. "Indeed. Death is always an unhappy affair."

Zhong cleared his throat. "Well, what do you think, Yan-du? Might there be a relationship or not?"

"Could be. Maybe not."

"That's not very helpful, sir," the security team leader muttered and shook his head.

"I think he means that we need to talk to the Taoist who

wrote the talisman and discover who else may have a similar tattoo," Xiang-hua, who couldn't resist explaining, said.

"That we'll do," Zhong replied, settling the cloth back onto the victim and casting a glance at Shi, who hovered nearby.

At hearing the gist of the conversation, Shi pulled himself up to his full height and threw back his shoulders. "Don't go looking at me. I know what you're up to. You want to pin this on me so that the magistrate thinks you're doing such a great job. Perhaps you're hoping he'll give you a reward. Maybe a job at the yamen where you can rake in money by squeezing so-called fees out of the innocent. But you can't blame me! I'm not a gang member. I don't know this fellow. I've never seen him in my life." His voice again rose as he ranted on.

Zhong's eyes burned with irritation and anger. He spat out a challenge. "It's mighty strange that this fellow's in your pigpen, being eaten by your pig. If that peddler hadn't been passing and seen the body, your pig might have eaten the whole thing and no one would be the wiser."

Xiang-hua took a step forward to intervene, but a hand grasped her just above the elbow. Her father. Preventing her from acting out. She looked back and forth from Shi to Zhong and waited.

"If you're so innocent, show us your left arm," Zhong demanded.

Shi laughed and pulled up his sleeve, exposing unmarked, brown skin. He spun around, so everyone could see. "Is that good enough?" With a grin of defiance, he thrust his arm forward and his sleeve flipped back into place.

"That settles it," he crowed. "No tattoo because I'm not a gangster. Ha. You thought you could tie me to this fellow, but you can't. I had nothing to do with this stranger ending up on my property." Shi thrust a finger toward Zhong. "I told you what happened. It's obvious. He wandered in here after being in a tavern brawl. Totally random. He could have ended up in my neighbor Rui Yao-sheng's yard." He waved broadly toward his neighbor's almost identical pigpen. "It was bad fate that brought the fellow here. But that's not a criminal offense." He shook a finger at Zhong. "You'll look like a fool if you take this to the magistrate." He whirled around to Xiang-hua. "And you, too, young lady," he sneered.

"And don't expect me to pay you *guanxi* to keep me out of court. I'll bring charges against you, either of you, if you do that."

Xiang-hua's cheeks grew hot. Shi's words bore down on her. He was implying that they were asking for a "gift" to keep his name out of their report to the court. The assault on her and her family infuriated her. "How dare—"

Before she could say more, her father's hand tightened on her arm. Swallowing hard, she clenched her fists and stepped back. With effort, she relaxed her hands and mouth. She didn't want others to see her inner turmoil.

"You're upset by this affair, Shi, and confused. I'm looking for what happened. As head of the town's security team, I'm answerable to the magistrate and, through him, to the emperor. It's critical to discover the chain of events leading up to this death and address it. That's all. No one is blaming you," Zhong said. If his words were meant to sooth Shi, his tone negated the effort. He couldn't hide his exasperation with the herbalist and his behavior.

"Right. That's right. Just don't think you can blame me. Remember, I have friends in the provincial city. I will destroy anyone who tries to implicate me," Shi said, lowering his head like a charging bull and staring at Xiang-hua.

CHAPTER 7

Peering beyond the clusters of curious people populating the road adjacent to Shi's, Shu-chang spotted Xiang-hua, Chu, and the security team leader. They were in close discussion with the herbalist, who suddenly turned and stomped into his house.

Shu-chang anxiously examined Xiang-hua's expression. He expected to find her pale and withdrawn after dealing with such a horrifying death. Instead, her cheeks flushed and her eyes flashed as she watched Shi close the door behind him. Shu-chang almost grinned. Perhaps he should have been worried about his anxiety, not hers.

Shifting his attention from concern for Xiang-hua to the scene of Shi's abrupt departure, he shot a questioning glance at Uncle Xin.

"Something just happened and we're in time to find out what it was," Xin said.

Shu-chang nodded. They picked up their pace. Curiosity drove them through the crowd and into the yard.

Shu-chang greeted the trio as he approached, his gaze lingering on Xiang-hua a moment longer than the others.

Zhong stepped in front of the covered corpse and welcomed them. "I guess you heard what happened."

"Just that a man was found dead, probably murdered," Uncle Xin said, looking past him toward the shrouded body.

"Gossip flies faster than a swallow," Shu-chang noted. "No doubt the entire village knows of this tragedy by now. Look at your spectators." He waved a hand towards the street. "Can't blame them. It might even help. Do you know who the fellow was?"

"Not yet. Shi claims he never saw him before."

"Then hopefully one of the gossips will be able to identify him," Shu-chang said.

Zhong wrinkled his brow and cast a strained glance at him. The case was already taking a toll on the older fellow. Usually in a small town like Jian, the most a security chief had to deal with was an exuberant drunk.

"People know an unidentified man has died. If someone in the family or neighborhood is missing, certainly they will come forward with that information," Uncle Xin said.

"Ah. I hope so. That would move things along." But Zhong's face suggested he wasn't convinced.

"What did you discover in inspecting the body?" Shu-chang asked Xiang-hua.

Before she could answer, however, a voice from behind them interrupted: "Sister Xiang-hua, you are needed at Master Xin Fen-peng's house. His wife, Lady Jiang, is not well."

They twisted around as one to face the speaker. A skinny, slumped man wearing a thread-bare jacket over his white breeches had entered the sty. He stood ringing his hands. "She needs you," he said, his voice low and his troubled expression fixed on the young doctor.

Fen-peng. She peered over at the spectators. Lady Jiang's husband had been among them earlier but no longer appeared in the crowd. She picked up her bag and turned to the newcomer. "Certainly," she said. "I'm finished here." She cast a last look at the shrouded figure. "I'll need to return home to renew my medicine bag. Tell Master Fen-peng that I will be there as soon as possible."

"I'll go with you," Chu said.

"You don't have to leave. It won't take me long," she said to her father.

"I'll go," he repeated firmly. "You may need assistance getting past those gawkers. They might try to accost you on your way back."

"I don't believe there will be any trouble," she said. "I've never had problems with people on the street."

"You never know. The victim was likely a gang member. Others in his gang may be among the spectators," her father said.

Shu-chang wanted to escort Xiang-hua back but resisted saying anything because he was sure she wouldn't accept his offer. He glanced at Chu, glad her father insisted on accompanying her through the crowd and to the house.

Xiang-hua's mouth tightened slightly in annoyance. Nevertheless, she nodded to the others and hurried away with her father. The crowd quietly parted as they approached, letting them pass through.

Shu-chang gazed after her slender figure disappearing down the road. She constantly surprised and mystified him. She wasn't like any other young woman he'd known in his village. Nevertheless, medical family or not, she shouldn't be out examining dead bodies; she should be home perfecting more womanly skills. He shook his head as he watched them leave. It's not that he didn't admire her. He did. But he worried for her future.

As he pivoted back toward the house, Uncle Xin caught his eye. "She's a remarkable woman," he said and smiled.

Shu-chang dodged the remark by quickly questioning the team leader. "Who is this Lady Jiang?" he asked.

"She married Xin Fen-peng some years ago. No children. She comes from a scholarly family in Nanchang. Although only in her forties, her virtue is already renowned in our town," Zhong said. "Fen-peng's family did well to arrange his marriage with her."

Shu-chang resumed his discussion with Zhong about the case. "Rumor is that you suspect this is murder."

Zhong pursed his lips and nodded. "Could be murder wasn't intended, but with a knife in the back, that doesn't seem likely."

"Well then, when you make out the official report for the magistrate, I'd be honored to help in any way I can." Shu-chang shifted his weight and leaned back on his feet. He didn't want to embarrass the team leader by mentioning the man's rudimentary education. It would be quite a challenge for him, if not impossible, to produce a proper formal document for the court.

A look of relief crossed Zhong's face. "Good. That's good. No hurry though. We won't be sending a report until tomorrow—or maybe the next day."

"What? Shouldn't one go out right away so the magistrate can begin his investigation?" Uncle Xin said.

"Normally. But Shi is making a case that the death could have been unintentional. It's not likely, but we have to consider it. Shi's claiming the man could have been in a drunken brawl, got hurt, staggered away, and accidentally fell into the sow's pen on his way home. Unable to get up, he could have bled out and died. Although still a punishable offense, if it wasn't truly deliberate murder, our town will look like a fool to His Honor. We could suffer consequences if he decides we've unnecessarily wasted the court's time because of poor judgement on our part. Not to mention we don't have the most basic information on the victim, much less the attacker. All in all, as it stands, I think it's too early to send a report to the court. One or two more days should give us a better picture to present to the magistrate."

"Hmm, I see what you mean," Uncle Xin said. He scratched his jaw. "It's best to get everything as perfect as possible before involving the provincial court."

"I'll ask around the neighborhood. I might be able to discover the fellow's identification," Zhong said. He glanced at the victim, paused, and frowned. "Of course, besides a name, it would sure help if someone could tell me definitively whether this guy was a gang member or not."

Shu-chang agreed. The government was particularly concerned about the existence and ongoing activities of gangs. Any gang had the potential of growing into a force powerful enough to control whole regions of the country. "I would be glad to help with the interviewing," Shu-chang volunteered.

"I wouldn't want to take you away from your teaching," Zhong said, casting a quick glance at Xin.

"I've dismissed my class for the day; the students have assignments to complete for tomorrow. I could spend the afternoon assisting."

"Yes, indeed. He could manage both," Uncle Xin said.

"Ah, I see. Yes. It would make quicker work with you helping. If you have the time," Zhong said to be polite. But his eyes were bright and his voice audibly relieved. "Besides the neighbors, I was also thinking we should check over on Shou Road. That's a warren of thieves for sure. A natural rat hole for gang members. We may find out something about this fellow's identity and background." He paused and passed a hand over his chin. "Of course, it might be dangerous for any of us to turn up there and go about asking questions."

"I happen to know a few men who live there," Shu-chang said, "I could check that out for you."

Zhong looked at him in surprise. A teacher who is familiar with thugs?

Shu-chang laughed. "It's not what you think. I met some workers who are from Fujian. They needed a place to stay, so they found cheap quarters on Shou Road. They're not thugs." *I hope*, Shu-chang added to himself.

As the three discussed their next moves, a burly man emerged from the neighboring residence and strode over. He opened the courtyard's gate and approached them.

"So, a dead man was found on the herbalist's property. I'm not surprised," he said as he came up and cast a baleful look at the corpse.

"You expected it?" Shu-chang asked, intrigued by the fellow's comment.

"This is Gao Yao-sheng, Shi's neighbor," Zhong said to Shu-chang. Then, facing Yao-sheng directly, he said: "What do you know about this?"

"Just that Shi's always arguing with someone. He's a difficult person."

Further amazed at the man's accusatory statements, Shu-chang asked: "Do you know the victim?"

Yao-sheng twitched and shoved his chin out. "How can I know who it is? He's covered with a sheet."

Zhong stepped over to the body. He pulled back the covering, revealing the man's mutilated face.

Yao-sheng followed his movement, briefly peered at it, grimaced, and nodded. "I can't tell you his name, but I saw him arguing with the herbalist just yesterday. Here. In the yard."

"That's a lie!" Shi yelled, stomping out of his house. He'd apparently been behind his latticed windows, listening the whole time. "I've never seen this fellow before!"

"That's what I would expect you to say," Yao-sheng sneered. He looked at Shu-chang and the others and wagged his head as if in disbelief. Then he shouted at the herbalist: "Prove it!"

At that, Shi's face turned a deep purple. He sputtered, unable to respond.

"It's impossible to prove a negative," Shu-chang said. He couldn't contain himself. He wasn't trying to defend Shi; it's just that it was true.

Yao-sheng shot the teacher a belligerent look and spun around toward the security chief. "You should arrest Shi on suspicion of killing this poor man."

Zhong raised his shoulders as if it wasn't up to him. "Impossible. I've no reason to arrest Shi. We don't even know the basics in the case yet."

"It's imperative that we discover the victim's identity and what caused his death," Shu-chang added.

"If you let that criminal go," Yao-sheng pointed a finger at the herbalist and then—pugnaciously eyeing each man—spat out, "you'll answer to the Emperor yourself. You'll not only be disgraced, you'll find yourself condemned for collusion!" With that, he whirled around and marched out of the yard.

Watching him go, Shu-chang stiffened. Why was there so much hostility radiating from these two men? Was all this blustering a screen? If so, who was hiding what?

A chill ran up Shu-chang's back. Involvement in this case would require great care. Yao-sheng was right. The emperor, and therefore the court, would not tolerate mistakes. His future could end before it began. There would be no passing the third level of national examinations and moving through its gateway and onto a successful career with status and position. No achieving his father's dream. No discovery of his father's and uncle's murderers. A complete and total failure of Shu-chang's filial duty.

CHAPTER 8

Chu remained home attending to a business matter, allowing his daughter to walk unaccompanied to Lady Jiang's.

After donning her large, woven grass hat, she hurried from the compound and through the streets, her medical bag clasped under her arm. A light breeze cleaned the town air. She took a deep breath, filling her lungs, and smiled. A sense of contentment at being out on her own, attending to patients who needed her, permeated every cell in her body. She appreciated that her father was torn between wanting to protect her and accepting her grandparents' choice in her education. He fretted over the implications for her life. Yet, he could never go against his parents' wishes.

Pushing onward, she picked up her pace. She wasn't worried. This was her life and she embraced it with a sense of satisfaction nothing else gave her. Xiang-hua shifted the weight of her bag and walked on.

Without knowing who was sick or what the symptoms were, her first thought was that Lady Jiang might be in imminent danger. She had rushed back to her lab, pushed by a sense of urgency; she couldn't afford to waste time. Now, however, her way was slowed by people filling the streets, most casually standing about, chatting. She pursed her lips and shook her head as she glanced at the clusters of gossipers. Lady Jiang's home was not far from the herbalist Shi's, and the excitement of the mysterious death had brought the curious out.

On the streets, a few of her fellow travelers greeted her as she dashed along. Many—having already learned through gossip that she acted as the coroner this morning—tried to pull her into a discussion about the death, but she didn't allow herself to be sidetracked by their idle curiosity.

Soon, a large but decrepit gate loomed ahead. Although it had once been painted a brilliant vermilion, that had long faded into a soft, uneven reddish-orange. Xiang-hua grasped the ring of a brass knocker and slammed it against the metal base.

A servant opened the door enough to peer out. At seeing Xiang-hua, he threw the door wide. "Ah, Sister. Lady Jiang is expecting you," he said, inviting her into a dusty courtyard.

Trees in large clay vessels graced one side, and several other potted leafy plants huddled together in an opposite corner. Not a leaf or twig marred the smooth, well-swept ground. A thin veranda ran around three sides of the court-yard. The warmth of the sun encouraged the well-cared for plants to offer up a pleasing, subtle fragrance. In spite—or because—of its simplicity, an aura of calm pervaded the space.

He led her to an inside door where he knocked. A maid-servant, looking to be at least her grandmother's age, imme-diately opened the door.

At seeing the doctor, the women's anxious face smoothed into a welcome. "Come in, come in. You're expected." Her words echoed the old man's.

Xiang-hua entered directly into the main reception area of the house. As with the outside, this room had seen better days. It was spacious, with parallel lines of dark, carved, wood armchairs lining the longer walls. An immense horizontal painting of the Eight Immortals stretched along one side behind a group of chairs. While the lines of chairs faced each other, their placement had the effect of immediately drawing the visitor's attention to the center-back of the room. There —on the wall opposite the main door—was the family's ancestral altar.

Not unlike the altar in her own home, this one was high, shallow, and wide. Its surface, polished from years of use, glowed in the room's muted light. A wooden plaque honored each of the family's immediate ancestors. Lit candles flickered on each side of the altar, and a bowl of fresh fruit sat front and center before the tablets. It looked like someone had been petitioning the ancestors.

Xiang-hua hesitated as she took in the room.

"Please sit, Sister. I'll tell Lady Jiang you've arrived." Pausing only long enough to be sure Xiang-hua was comfortable, the maid disappeared through a side door.

Soon, a thin woman appeared in the doorway. Everything about her exuded elegant restraint: her hair was pulled back in a bun, and she wore a dark, unadorned dress with a long tunic embroidered along its lapel and hem. The cotton fabric was finely made but also showed signs of careful mending on the sleeves and front collar. This finding confirmed Xiang-hua's burgeoning suspicion that this once-wealthy household was undergoing hard times.

Entering the room, Lady Jiang limped slightly, as if in pain. On seeing the young doctor, however, she perked up and gushed a warm welcome.

"Sister Xiang-hua. I'm glad you were able to come so quickly. I understand your grandmother is at the capital. That speaks well of her great and many skills. Which I'm sure she passed on to you," she added.

Xiang-hua bowed. "You are more than kind, Lady Jiang. I can only try to live up to her expectations." Politeness required her to be modest, but it was easy to be modest when standing in the shadow of her grandmother's reputation. On the one hand, clients trusted Xiang-hua's treatments—even though she was young and had only been working on her own since her grandmother left for the capital. On the other hand, she wondered if she would ever be able to live up to her responsibilities.

She looked up at this slender, almost gaunt, woman. The local gentry and townspeople lauded her virtue as a daughter-in-law and wife. Xiang-hua could only hope that, with unstinting work, she could meet the expectations such a remarkable woman had of her.

After tea and chit-chat, Lady Jiang broached her mother-in-law's health rather than mentioning her own condition. Since the messenger had only said Lady Jiang needed a doctor, she hadn't expected to treat Fen-peng's mother as well. That Lady Jiang would want Xiang-hua to treat her mother-in-law first demonstrated the filial piety she was so famous for.

Xiang-hua leaned slightly forward in her chair and listened carefully as Lady Jiang began to enumerate her mother-in-law's symptoms. The young doctor had learned over the years of her apprenticeship that her first task was to gather as much information about the patient as she could from the family. They were the most familiar with the patients' medical histories as well as their current problems. Listening was critical for forming a competent diagnosis.

"My mother-in-law appears to sleep well, yet is constantly tired. Listlessness. I guess that's how I'd describe it. It's so unlike her."

"How long has she been like that?"

"Oh," Lady Jiang lightly touched her chin with her index finger, thinking. "It's been a while. Perhaps a few weeks. She didn't want to bother with a doctor when she thought changing her diet and taking other herbs would help in time." She glanced away, then back again. "However, I didn't want to wait any longer to call in your services. She seems more accepting of seeing a doctor now that I've already contacted you."

"Hmm. Have you noticed any other changes? Is she more thirsty or hungry than usual?"

"No. She's never mentioned being thirsty. I do give her hot water and green tea, but she drinks it only because I give it to her. As for food—" She shook her head. "Really, I think she'd never eat if I didn't sit with her and make sure she had something."

"How about pain? Has she complained about any discomfort?"

"She has some trouble walking when she first stands up. Once she starts moving, though, she's fine. She's been like that for years," Lady Jiang said. "What concerns me is that she complains about always being chilled, even though I keep a brazier going at all times."

"That can be expensive," Xiang-hua said.

"Yes. But I want her to be comfortable," Lady Jiang said with a pensive glance at the adjoining door.

Tucking this information away, Xiang-hua asked to see Lady Jiang's mother-in-law. Lady Jiang rose and led her into a neatly appointed room. From her position behind the house's mistress, Xiang-hua again noted her slight limp.

Stuffy, dry air engulfed them as they entered the bedroom. The wood-and-paper lattice windows were tightly shut against the outside, and a brazier set close to the opposite wall glowed. The temperature in the room was stifling.

"Mother, I've brought Sister Xiang-hua to see you," Lady Jiang softly said in the direction of a tiny figure curled up on the kang under a mound of blankets.

The elderly woman stirred, pushing the blankets away from her head and sitting up. Blurry eyes settled on the young doctor. "Ah, Sister. How is your grandmother? Is she well?" she asked in a paper-thin voice.

Xiang-hua stepped close to the kang and talked briefly about her grandmother, explaining why she wasn't the one to come and attend to her.

"Sister Xiang-hua has taken care of many of our friends, mother. Her grandmother did a good job training her in the medical arts."

The older woman nodded and had started to recline once more when she covered her mouth as if she were going to cough. Lady Jiang jumped up and grabbed a shallow basin, placing it under her mother-in-law's chin just as she spit out a pale, watery substance.

Holding the basin in one hand, Lady Jiang offered her mother-in-law a handkerchief. The woman's hand trembled slightly as she took it and wiped her chin. She lay down again with a sigh.

Xiang-hua bent over her and gently took her hand. Placing three fingers on the woman's wrist, Xiang-hua read her pulse. It was feeble. Placing the hand down on the kang and covering it with the blanket, she observed the resting elder who lay with her eyes open, fixed on the doctor. Her breathing was short and shallow.

While it was not unusual for people to become more fragile as they aged, Lady Jiang's mother-in-law's condition appeared more severe. On the other hand, she expressed interest in Xiang-hua's family and in gossip about the town. This interest in the world outside her compound's walls encouraged the young doctor. It indicated that her patient's mind was still sharp—even though her body was failing her.

Xiang-hua rummaged in her medicine bag and pulled out a container of salve, a tiny ball of mugwort, and a small cup. After applying moxibustion to the elder woman's lower back, she left the room, allowing her to rest.

She returned to the main reception area with Lady Jiang and handed her a small bag of crushed herbs. "Put one spoonful of this into a cup of hot water three times a day and give it to your mother-in-law to drink," Xiang-hua said. "Also, she needs to have soup daily, one that is made with chicken or pork. Make sure she eats the meat as well as drinks the liquid. If you can do it, she should also have an egg each day."

Lady Jiang's shoulders sagged slightly. She stroked her right leg as she nodded. "I'll do all that I can."

"And how are you doing?" Xiang-hua asked. Lady Jiang's leg concerned her. Something was clearly wrong.

"I'm fine. Never better. As you may have heard, Fen-peng is home. His presence has been a great comfort to his mother."

"I saw your husband earlier today. I'm glad he's back from his travels," Xiang-hua said.

"Yes. His business often takes him away for months at a time. He was gone a whole year on this last trip. He returned just last week. It's good to have him home again. His mother missed him terribly." She smiled tentatively.

Xiang-hua wondered why her smile looked strained if it truly was good to have him home.

"You know how mothers are: they always worry about what their sons are up to, no matter their ages."

"It's an occupational hazard," Xiang-hua agreed.

"Where did you see him?" Lady Jiang casually asked, although Xiang-hua thought she detected a note of anxiety in her voice.

"A man was found dead and Fen-peng was among the observers on the street."

Lady Jiang's head snapped up, her face pale and her eyes wide. "Who was it? Where did it happen? Was Fen-peng involved?"

"It looks like the man was an outsider, not from our town," Xiang-hua said. She wondered why Lady Jiang asked if her husband had been involved. Why would he be? "At least, no one claims to know him," she continued. "His body was found at the herbalist Shi's place. I was there as the coroner. That's where I saw your husband, standing amongst the street crowd who came to see what was happening."

Lady Jiang sank down, but she looked less anxious.

"Are you okay? Is something bothering you?"

Lady Jiang straightened up. "No. No," she said in a distracted voice.

"If you're not well, I can help," Xiang-hua repeated. She was sure if there was a problem, she could help with it. *When will people trust me the way they do my grandmother?*

"It's just something silly." Lady Jiang shook her head. "Since he's returned home, my husband has been unsettled. Upset with the herbalist."

Xiang-hua raised her eyebrows.

Lady Jiang laughed nervously and looked away. After a moment, she continued: "For the past few months, I've been buying herbs from Master Shi. For my mother-in-law. To build up her strength." She was about to add more, appeared to decide against it, and paused again.

Xiang-hua nodded. Before seeking a doctor, using herbs was the first line of defense against illness. Although they could be expensive, anyone who could afford it would most certainly buy them. And, of course, such care was demanded as a filial duty for one's parents or a wife's in-laws. It's what she would expect from Lady Jiang.

After another nervous laugh, Lady Jiang added, "Unfortunately, when Fen-peng discovered that Master Shi frequently visited—bringing the herbs directly to me—he became upset. Accused me of being enamored with Master Shi. Of course, that's completely unreasonable. How could he even consider such a thing? But my husband has fixated on the idea." She looked at Xiang-hua and held her gaze. "Please. Don't mention this to anyone. I don't want people gossiping about our family."

Xiang-hua agreed. She very much wanted to know more about Fen-peng's obsession with the herbalist, but she was sure that any inquiries at this time would alienate Lady Jiang. Before leaving, she promised to return the next day to see how her mother-in-law was doing. She didn't mention the obvious problem Lady Jiang was having walking. She intended to learn more about that tomorrow as well.

CHAPTER 9

S hi's neighbor marched back to his yard and disappeared into the house, leaving Shu-chang, Uncle Xin, and the security team leader behind in a stunned silence, his hostile outburst still ringing in their ears.

Finally, Shu-chang shook his head and shrugged. What was there to say? Did Yao-sheng's unprovoked rancor imply something sinister or was it merely an opportunity to be-smudge his more prosperous neighbor's reputation?

"I'm sure you've checked the area thoroughly, but if you don't mind, I'd also like to have a look around," Shu-chang said to the security chief.

Zhong, his eyes still on Yao-sheng's closed door, nodded.

"I'd better get back to work. I've been gone too long already, and the morning is fleeting." Uncle Xin said and turned to Shu-chang, "I'll see you later. Come to my office when you get home."

"I will," Shu-chang said. "It'll be a while, though. I want to talk to possible witnesses, before they forget what they saw. Or have time to create alternate scenarios. Hopefully, we'll be able to gather accurate information."

"Right," Uncle Xin said. He nodded curtly to each man and left, his robe flapping behind him.

Outside the muddy sty, Shu-chang examined the wall, gate, and ground around it for signs of a struggle or drag marks. After vigilantly and cautiously scrutinizing every nook and cranny, the wall refused to yield anything useful. Nothing.

Shoving away the disappointment, he scanned the pen's exterior once more. While the wall wouldn't speak to him, he hoped the bare earth would. If the body had been carried or dragged over and then dumped in with the pigs, there should be telltale marks in the dirt indicating where the murder had happened.

The number of onlookers had diminished. Zhong and the rest of his men, save the one who stood over the corpse, had left. The call of lunch was more powerful than their curiosity about this unusual death.

He eventually found a set of vague, yet potentially useful, marks down the middle of the road between the deeply embedded wagon ruts. Despite being interrupted and partially obscured by the many footprints left by the day's crowd, the marks suggested something large had been dragged from the street to the wall. Shu-chang bent down for a closer look. He was sure this was it—or, at least, he hoped it was.

At the point where the disturbed dirt ended, he peered over the waist-high wall. The body was found directly on the other side. His blood surged. Too bad Zhong and his men had already moved on. The one guard left behind squatted nearby, nodding drowsily.

The corpse lay on the board, mute. But Shu-chang felt its spirit, which refused to rest.

No, he thought. *It isn't mute. It's demanding justice.*

Shu-chang shivered. This stranger had met a violent,

unexpected death, just like his own father and uncle. He stared hard at the lumpy, cloth-covered form.

"I'll do everything I can. I promise," he whispered and turned back to the disturbed soil.

The faint trail led from Shi's courtyard and to the left, toward town. Fortunately, this section had little traffic. While the marks sometimes disappeared beneath newly churned earth, he was able to pick them up again. Slowly, vigilantly, he studied the ground. He tracked the drag marks until he arrived at a cross-road near a maze of hovels. The foot and cart traffic intensified here, obliterating the path he'd been following. He'd lost the trail.

Straightening, he found himself on Shou Road. Poorly constructed, badly worn buildings lined the intersecting lane to his left. This corner of town accepted all comers and never questioned their past or present occupations. It was infamous for being infested with vagabonds and criminals interspersed with the poor. A tough neighborhood.

Nevertheless, the daily pattern of life was as lively here as anywhere in the town. Petty merchants wheeled their carts down the street, avoiding peddlers who sold their wares and foods out of large baskets dangling at the end of poles balanced on their shoulders. Old men lounged against walls and chatted quietly. Further down the lane, a noisy, raucous group surrounded a cluster of men squatting on the ground and gambling. The audience loudly called out to the players as the game proceeded, either encouraging or disparaging them.

Shu-chang yawned broadly and casually gazed around the street. What to do? Where to start? As he feigned what he hoped was a disinterested, unthreatening pose, a drunk staggered down the road and fell onto him. He turned his face toward Shu-chang's in an attempt to recognize the man he'd stumbled into. Shu-chang gaged at his foul breath and jerked back.

Seeing a man in a long robe, the drunk slurred out an "I'm sorry, sir" as he teetered toward the teacher again.

Simultaneously pushing him away and stepping further off the road, Shu-chang pressed up against the side of a shop. Without another word, the drunk lumbered on. If this was what he'd run into on the warren's outskirts, what would he find inside?

Under the building's low-hanging roof, Shu-chang relaxed. From this vantage point, he could study the street scene more carefully while formulating his next steps. The dead man very likely would have spent time here. Whether he lived in the warren or not was another matter. And whether anyone would admit to knowing him was yet another. Surely everyone had already learned about the death of an unidentified man. It'd been hours since the body was found. Yet, so far, no one came forward to say their husband, brother, son, or friend was missing.

Mulling these things over, he absently watched the rowdy knot of men. An eruption of laughter signaled the game's end. The tight circle of observers jostled one another. A fresh group of gamblers took the place of men leaving the game. Unexpectedly, a familiar form rose from the ground and joined the circle of on-lookers. Xiao-ren.

With a snort of irritation, Shu-chang thrust himself away from the wall. He marched into the infamous warren, his temper rising at every step. Xiao-ren wasn't just his younger cousin, he was Shu-chang's student. A student in the Xin clan's school. Every Xin member would hold Shu-chang responsible for his pupil's indecent behavior. Without question. A teacher's responsibilities were more than simply making sure his students knew how to read and write properly. The teacher also encouraged and developed his students' character and sense of moral rectitude. If Xiao-ren's behavior did not reflect such lessons, it was because his teacher had not taught them well enough.

The sight of Xiao-ren carrying on in the streets with a bunch of ruffians made Shu-chang tremble with anger. Is this what he did when he left the house? He was supposed to be doing his assignment. He'd said he would. So why wasn't he?

Shu-chang bore down on the noisy group with the righteous wrath of Guan Gong, god of justice and war. Reaching the boisterous circle before anyone noticed him, he caught Xiao-ren by the collar and unceremoniously hauled him out and away from his fellow gamblers.

Xiao-ren frantically slapped at the iron-grip that held him, cursing and futilely attempting to turn his head to bite the attacker's arm. Seeing him being accosted by a man in a teacher's long robe, the men around the youth roared in laughter.

Shu-chang dragged his flailing captive away from the rowdy group before whirling him around.

As soon as Xiao-ren saw his assailant, he metamorphosed from a hooligan into a supplicant, dropping his aggressive stance as his face turned bright red. He clasped his hands in front of him and began to frantically bow, going lower each time.

"That won't get you off so easily," Shu-chang said, his voice tense with anger.

Xiao-ren ducked his head. "Teacher. I apologize. I didn't know it was you."

"Just what do you think you are doing? You were late for class this morning, and now I find you've lied to me again. You're not attending to your lessons. Instead, what do I find? Here you are—gambling and carousing in the streets. Wasting your life."

"It's ... I—"

"Don't talk! How dare you! How are you ever going to repay your father? You're throwing away the life he gave you! You're insolent. Unworthy. You've been given so much. All you show is disrespect."

Xiao-ren hung his head in shame. Shu-chang's yelling brought swift glances from passersby, but no one stopped. Arguments and fights held out in the open were not unusual in this quarter. Most people just wanted to stay out of it. No one needed more trouble, especially from someone they didn't even know. A bubble of space formed around the two as the locals cautiously moved past them through the narrow alley.

Xiao-ren dropped to his knees, bowing. "Teacher, forgive me. I was careless. Stupid. Unfilial."

Seeing Xiao-ren bowing and apologizing mitigated some of Shu-chang's anger. Still, the teacher in him hesitated to relent. If he didn't learn his lessons young, he'd only get worse as he got older. At the same time, now that the roiling fury had abated, the youth in Shu-chang found it difficult to keep up his diatribe.

With a sharp exhalation, he managed to say through tight lips: "All right. All right! Get up."

Xiao-ren rose and stood in front of him, eyes down.

"Go home. I'll talk to you later."

"Will you tell father?" the chastised young man asked, his voice begging for a "no."

Shu-chang stared at him for a long time before relenting. "No. I won't say anything. But don't expect leniency in the future."

Although the look of contrition remained on Xiao-ren's face, his shoulders straightened and his chin lifted.

"I never want to find you here gambling in the streets again. Do you understand?"

The boy rapidly nodded in quick agreement. A grin flashed across his face, but he quickly squashed it with a hand over his mouth. He started to turn to go.

"I expect you'll perfect tomorrow's lesson. You'll be the first to recite."

Xiao-ren gave another low bow and fled.

After watching his student dash down the alley and disappear out on the main road, Shu-chang returned to his original task. His heart sank as he looked around and found he was standing in the middle of the warren. In his fury, he hadn't noticed he'd entered this dangerous labyrinth of houses.

He surveyed the area. An old man squatted alone in an entranceway, gazing out at the passing people through half-closed eyes. Well, this unintimidating observer was as good a starting point as he was likely to find. Shu-chang smoothed his sleeves and started toward the man. The elderly often proved to be the most reliable eyes and ears of a neighborhood.

Before taking more than a couple of steps, a massive shadow moved in front of Shu-chang. Without taking his eyes off his target, he automatically stepped aside to let the stranger pass. His mind remained focused on how he should approach the old fellow.

The stranger's movements mirrored his own. Still lost in thought, Shu-chang stepped aside once more. The form moved again. Too late Shu-chang realized the massive shape was purposely blocking his way. He halted abruptly, wondering if there was still time to avoid this new problem.

But no. It looked like confrontation was unavoidable.

Inhaling deeply, he gathered his strength and slowly looked upward, bracing for the worst.

CHAPTER 10

Expecting a fight—not at all what he wanted—Shu-chang raised his hands, stepped back, and stood firmly. The added space allowed him to use his legs as weapons. He hardened his facial expression, hoping it made him look tough, and raised his head to take in the powerfully built, domineering man before him.

Upon seeing the fellow's face, however, Shu-chang dropped his stance. A grin replaced his grim, compressed lips. "Zhou, what a surprise!" He warmly greeted the man he was prepared to fight a moment before.

He'd met Zhou and his two friends not long ago. They were outsiders from a nearby province. A rough-and-tumble trio. Nevertheless, when Shu-chang and Xiang-hua had been unexpectedly confronted with a complicated arson and murder case, they had proved to be reliable and trustworthy allies.

"Same here, Teacher," the big fellow returned with a toothy smile. "I didn't know this was your sort of place." He swept a hand toward the ramshackle houses.

"I'm looking to identify a man," Shu-chang said.

Zhou threw his hands up, as if pushing something away, and raised his eyebrows. "Don't tell me you're involved with that murdered fellow in the pigsty?"

Shu-chang nodded. "It's a wretched affair. What have you heard about it?"

"Just that a body was discovered half eaten by a sow ... and that the security team thinks it's murder."

Shu-chang surveyed the street. "No gossip about who the victim might be?"

Zhou looked down the alley and moved his hands behind his back. "None."

His body language wasn't lost on Shu-chang. "This won't get anyone in trouble. I'm only looking for information."

"Yeah. About a murderer."

"We don't want a killer running around our streets, do we? He killed once. What's to stop him from killing again?"

Zhou studied a worn sign hanging askew in front of a store across the street, its characters so badly worn they were almost indecipherable.

Shu-chang leaned slightly toward him and waited.

"I haven't heard much gossip. Really. It's mostly an elaboration of what you probably already know," he said. "Just that a man's dead."

"Any little bit of information could prove useful," Shu-chang encouraged.

Turning the ends of his mouth down, Zhou shifted his stance. "Well, in that case, I might know a place you might be interested in."

Shu-chang pricked up his ears. "Good. Where?" Finally, a crack in the door. His heart beat faster. Coming here had been a good idea.

"Ah. Can't say." Zhou looked away then back at him once more.

Shu-chang scowled.

Zhou hastily went on: "I know what you'll do. You can't go there. Look at your robe." He flicked a hand up and down. "Clearly you don't belong here. It's not safe. The people I know are not the friendly type."

Shu-chang paused, studying his friend's face. "Then you can take me."

Zhou heaved an exaggerated sigh. "Don't you know how to stay out of trouble? A gentleman like you shouldn't go meddling in things that don't concern him."

Shu-chang stifled a chuckle at being called a "gentleman." His job as teacher didn't pay much, but it immediately elevated his social status. His father would be proud.

"Take me there and you'll be rewarded." He didn't have any money; he was betting on Zhong or Uncle Xin being willing to cover whatever it took. After all, this was a community problem.

Zhou pulled himself up to his full height. "Don't mention it. You're a friend. Money isn't necessary between us."

"Thank you for your kindness. That means you'll take me, yes?" Shu-chang tilted his head and grinned.

"Bah," Zhou griped. "I'll take you, but first we should pick up my buddies."

Shu-chang nodded. He was glad Lin and Fang were still with Zhou. They would be excellent backup, if—as Zhou implied—it was needed.

They moved quickly down the alley, swerving here and there on the narrow thoroughfare to avoid carts and peddlers' poles. The dusty air enclosed them like a coffin. A discordant backdrop of voices calling out wares followed them. Everyone was out to make a living.

They soon came to a shabby building. Not that that distinguished it much from any other structure in the warren. Shabby was the neighborhood's defining characteristic. Nevertheless, the sturdy entrance door wore its scrapes, cuts, and gouges with pride. No telltale signage announced what business might be found inside. Zhou threw the door wide and strode in.

"Our abode," he said. "Simple, cheap, and clean enough."

The tavern showed pride of ownership: its floor had been cleaned, and the few tables and stools scattered in the tight space were free of debris. A middle-aged man, who looked like life had chewed him up and spit him out, stood behind a bar, holding a chipped bowl and scooping rice into his mouth. At the sight of the men, he paused, bowl in midair, appraising them. His eyes never left the two as they came forward, but he remained silent.

"Afternoon," Zhou said as he marched through the room towards a set of stairs at the back.

The man nodded, his eyes shifting to Shu-chang and lingering there.

Shu-chang returned the nod but didn't break his pace behind Zhou.

The thick, wooden stairs looked well-worn but solid. Zhou opened the first door on the landing, and they entered a tiny, darkened room. Inside, two men sprawled on a kang, playing a card game. They barely glanced up as Shu-chang and Zhou entered. At the sight of Shu-chang, however, they straightened up.

"Look who I found wandering our fair streets," Zhou said, sweeping a hand toward Shu-chang.

"Honorable Teacher," Lin and Fang said simultaneously, giving a short bow of their heads and upper shoulders.

"It's good to see you again," Shu-chang said. The two had the characteristic lean, muscular bodies of men used to hard labor.

His eyes adjusted to the gloomy room, allowing him to peer around. The wooden kang dominated the floor. To the right of the door, along the wall, stood a narrow, serviceable table with a large bowl. An undecorated chest sat on the other side of the door. These few pieces choked any free space out of the room.

"A couple of other men share our sleeping quarters." Zhou spread his hands out, as if encompassing the room. "Fortunately, they are out at the moment."

"They found work today," Lin volunteered. "Lucky for them," he added. A severe drought had decimated a nearby province, causing famine, death, and hardship. Thousands of men, bereft of their families, became dislocated. As with Zhou and his friends, they'd taken to the road and had traveled to Jian township seeking work. Too many came, making even small jobs hard to find.

Clearing his throat, Shu-chang said: "I've come to offer you three a job, if you'll take it."

Lin and Fang quickly nodded in agreement. They began to stand up, crowding the limited space even more.

Zhou held up his hand to slow their enthusiasm. "Teacher Shu-chang is working on that pigsty death. He wants us to take him around and assist in interviewing. Looking for information."

Fang's face dropped. He stared at Shu-chang and displayed his open, calloused hands. "If you wanted me to carry rocks, or fix a building, I could help." He turned his hands over and let them rest on his legs. "But, to be honest, Teacher, I'm not good at talking to people," he said, his brow furrowed in concentration as he thought through his words.

"Don't worry about that. That's not exactly what I had in mind."

Lin and Fang exchanged perplexed looks.

"You've not been here long, but I'd say long enough to know this neighborhood and its secrets," Shu-chang said.

The men nodded.

"On the other hand, as Zhou pointed out to me, I'm an

outsider. What I'd like is for you all to take me to the most likely places I'll meet people with any knowledge about the victim. Also, from what Zhou says," he nodded toward the big fellow, "I understand that the men I'll need to talk to might not be the most upright citizens. So I would like you to accompany me as I interview the locals."

"To act as a protector," Zhou added.

Shu-chang nodded.

At that, the two clambered off the kang and grabbed their jackets.

"Sounds like fun. It sure beats carrying rocks," Lin said, beaming. His grin revealed a missing front tooth. Fang grunted his agreement as he shrugged into his jacket and tied it with a thick cotton belt.

Pleased at their enthusiasm, Shu-chang clasped his hands together. This was going to work. He looked to Zhou and hesitated. He didn't exude the same zeal and was definitely holding back.

"Zhou?"

The big guy eyed his friends. "It's good for us to help Teacher, but I want to be clear about what we might be getting into. Remember: carrying rocks will give you a sore back and shoulders, but this job is much more dangerous. We may end up not just hurt, but dead."

Zhou's words were like a fist to his gut. Shu-chang couldn't disagree. Not after hearing Zhou's earlier assessment.

Nevertheless, he needed them and would be glad to have this trio of friends onboard. He had faith in his own ability to protect himself. Well, almost. He had to admit that his skill was limited. His childhood friend, Jin-fang, had taught him a few martial arts techniques in their home village. But only a few. Certainly not enough to allow him to be overconfident in his skills. He'd never be able to handle all opponents. Fortunately, while these three weren't skilled in the arts, they were skilled in street fighting. And that's exactly what they may need. If the murderer was from this neighborhood, the niceties of martial arts training would be moot.

"Not a problem. I could use some entertainment," Lin said with bravado.

"Same here," Fang said.

"Zhou, it looks like we're ready. What do you think?" Shu-chang said, hoping he wouldn't hold back.

Zhou shifted and nodded assent.

"Great. Where do we start?"

"I'm not sure, but from the local gossip, it sounds like your victim might have been a member of a gang working out of the Flying Crane. The wine shop's not too far from here," Zhou said.

"The White Feather Gang?" Lin asked, eyes wide. He shot a quick glance at Fang, who compressed his lips and shook his head.

"That's the one."

"Who're they?" Shu-chang asked.

"The most powerful gang in the region," Zhou said. "They're called 'White Feather' because members wear a small, white pigeon feather in their caps."

"Hmm," Shu-chang said. "What's the feather for?"

"It identifies a fellow gang member. At the same time, a small feather tucked into the hat isn't likely to draw attention from the uninitiated."

As Zhou spoke, Lin reached down into a bundle near him and removed a cord with a weight at each end. He dropped it into his jacket. The weapon could strangle an opponent when thrown around his neck. "I'm ready."

Fang reached into another bundle on the kang. He pulled out a knife, wiped it, and slipped it into his boot. "Me too," he said with a grin.

At the sight of their weapons, the reality of their task

finally fully hit the teacher. Shu-chang's throat went dry. *What am I getting them into?*

With another glance at Fang, who was pushing the knife further into his boot, Shu-chang shuddered. *What danger would they get him into?*

CHAPTER 11

Shu-chang was tempted to halt his investigation. He closed his eyes, and an image of a mutilated face, its flesh partly eaten away, swam into focus. He sucked in a shot of air. No one deserved such a death. He opened his eyes and looked at the men. "Let's go."

Newly determined, the four marched out of the room, down the stairs, through the wine shop, and out into the street where the sun struggled to brighten the dingy air caught between the rows of dilapidated buildings.

They strode purposefully toward their destination, Shu-chang and Zhou in front, Lin and Fang close behind. The lane was too narrow for them to walk four abreast.

As Zhou promised, they didn't have far to travel. They soon came to a more imposing and better kept structure than any of the neighboring shops and wine houses. An elaborate, freshly painted picture of a red-crowned crane cupped the characters naming the business: the Flying Crane."

Shu-chang allowed Zhou to enter first. Lin and Fang followed Shu-chang into a dim and raucous room with more than a dozen tables. A stairway led to an open gallery encircling the second floor. Multiple doors punctuated its walls. As the four entered, the noise dropped to a murmur. Shu-chang was painfully aware of numerous sets of eyes following their every movement.

The quartet ambled to an empty table against the front wall and sat. Shu-chang, mindful of his position in the group, raised his hand toward a gaunt man wearing an apron and standing near a table of customers. "Sir, tea for four."

The fellow nodded and slipped out of the room. He returned within moments, cups and pot in hand. As he placed them on the table, he asked: "Anything else? We have the best crispy pork in Jian."

"Good. Crispy pork with a plate of onions, roasted duck, hot and sour soup, and a bowl of rice," Shu-chang ordered.

Without another word, the man gave him a quick, short bow and left.

Zhou poured the tea. They drank in silence, each keeping attuned to the conversations and movements around them.

When the tavern-keeper returned with the various dishes, Shu-chang ordered another pot of tea. The three friends dug into the food with gusto. *When had they eaten last?* Shu-chang wondered as he watched the men. *Should I have ordered more?*

As his companions devoured their meal, Shu-chang surreptitiously peered around, examining each man in the room. An older patron, sitting at a table nearest the front door, caught his attention. Shu-chang adjusted his position on his stool, turning more directly toward Zhou, which gave him a clearer line of sight.

The old fellow stared straight ahead, never looking at his wine cup even when he reached for it. He seemed to share in the jokes and conversation without engaging any of the others directly. A staff rested against the wall behind his chair.

Shu-chang suddenly understood. The man was blind. Yet

he was treated with great respect by the other patrons. The young and middle-aged men who filled the room appeared to make it a point to stop at his table for a moment before moving on. Shu-chang raised an eyebrow as he cautiously continued to observe the table.

If gang members were among the men present, their deference toward this elderly, blind fellow improved Shu-chang's estimation of them. How despicable could a person be if he showed such respect toward the disabled?

Shu-chang shifted again to face out toward the majority of customers. As men sauntered past or sat at nearby tables, he sought out the telltale white feathers stuck into wearers' caps. He also tried to identify the leaders, as well as the weakest in each cluster. Both types might provide information he could use to create a complete picture of the why, who, and what in this case.

He sought out a possible nook or cranny to interview a likely candidate. His heart dropped. The room wasn't small, but it didn't offer any table isolated enough for a private conversation. Without legal authority in this matter, it would be difficult to entice anyone to come forward, especially if they had to do it in full view of the other patrons.

While Shu-chang mulled over his plan, a short, power-fully-built young man sauntered up to their table. He stopped a hand's distance from Shu-chang and stood towering over him with his feet spread wide apart. The young stranger wore the standard worker's outfit, but the cloth was of a finer weave, and the cut didn't look as casual and slipshod as most. He exuded authority. A quick peek at his soft hat revealed a discreet white feather tucked into its brim.

"Haven't seen you fellows around in a while," the newcomer said to Shu-chang's friends.

"Been busy. Found a bit of work. Didn't pay much, but it was work," Zhou said.

"This a workmate?" the stranger asked in a low, gravelly voice, as he eyed Shu-chang's long robe. The question was a not-so-subtle insult to a person of evident status.

"An old friend. Ran into him unexpectedly," Zhou said. "Teacher Shu-chang, this is He Da. He Da, Teacher Shu-chang."

Shu-chang, ignoring the proffered insolence, indicated an empty stool at the table. "Join us?" Without waiting for a response, he called over the tavern-keeper to order more tea, while his senses became even more alert. Keenly aware of other men in the room keeping them under scrutiny, he maintained an amicable tone. Were they now the main attraction because he and his friends were in trouble, or were the men interested simply because he was an outsider?

The tavern-keeper rushed over with a fresh pot. As he was about to set it down, He Da waved it away. "Not tea. Bring a jug of wine." His eyes burrowed into Shu-chang. "You have a problem with that?" he said as he sat.

Giving him an affable grin, Shu-chang said to the tavern keeper, "Wine will do."

The man scurried away, returning shortly with another cup and a jug of wine.

Shu-chang poured for everyone. taking up his cup in two hands, he called, "Gan bei!"

They all gulped the wine down.

He Da, his heavy lids shadowing his eyes, said to Shu-chang, "You look familiar. Been here before?"

Shu-chang shook his head. "I'm the Xin clan's new school teacher. I've only been in town a short time."

He Da nodded without comment, but Shu-chang could feel the weight of his stare under those hooded eyes. What did He Da know about him? Had he heard about his solving the warehouse case? Would that make the gangster more cautious or more aggressive?

Zhou cleared his throat. "Yeah, that's how we happened to run into him. Teacher found one of his students gambling at the entrance to the warren and was giving him what-for when we happened by."

He Da gave Shu-chang a crooked smirk that almost looked like a friendly grin. "Got to keep an eye on those young ones, don't we? If we didn't they'd get into mischief for sure. Maybe even join a gang. Very dangerous." He guffawed loudly.

His brazenness stung. Even talking about gangs and gang activities was frowned upon by the government. The Ming Emperor branded them all threats to his still fragile, newly established dynasty. Most citizens avoided mentioning the topic all together.

"Don't look so alarmed, Teacher," He Da said. "I'm sure your cubs won't stray so far away from the righteous path." And he laughed again with his unpleasant chortle.

"I'm not worried about them," Shu-chang said. "Nevertheless, they are boys, after all. It is my responsibility to make sure they are well-behaved." He poured more wine and invited He Da to drink.

He Da held his cup up in both hands, nodding toward Shu-chang and the others at the table. They all took up their cups in response. "Gan bei!" He Da called and downed his wine in one gulp, as did the others. Shu-chang threw his head back as if drinking the wine, but when he put his cup down he kept his hand over its brim, hiding the contents. He didn't want a clouded mind.

Zhou refilled all the cups once more, skimming lightly over Shu-chang's.

"This has been a troubling day," Shu-chang began as they all drank, "You've probably already heard about the man found dead in the herbalist's pigpen on Huang Lu road?"

"Who hasn't? Terrible thing. Hope they catch the turtle's

egg who did it," He Da said with feeling. "Man doesn't deserve such desecration after death. He shouldn't go into the afterlife maimed like that. His spirit will be angry, that's for sure. And want revenge on whoever did this." His hand tightened into a fist.

He Da's surge of anger was palpable.

Shu-chang clasped his wine cup and, looking into the clear liquid, offhandedly said, "So far the body's not been identified. Do you have any idea who it could be?" He looked up at He Da and held his eyes. "Is anyone missing that you know of?"

He Da, regrouping, cast an appraising glance around the room. "No idea." He called out into the crowded assemblage: "The Teacher wants to know if anyone's gone missing. He's trying to identify that dead man found this morning. Any ideas?"

The room's silence answered him. No one was willing to admit they had any knowledge. Throwing the question out to the gathering could have been He Da's way of helping them, but more likely it had been a warning to all that they should remain silent. After all, if their leader wasn't going to identify the man, they shouldn't either.

Despite his misgivings, Shu-chang nodded to placate his distrustful audience. He Da's reaction was out of proportion with what he'd expect if the victim had truly been a complete stranger. The dead man had a tattoo on his arm. The answer to who the man was clearly lay here, in this den of thieves. But how was he to get answers if no one opened up to him?

No more information was forthcoming from He Da or any of the men in the room. After finishing the jug of wine, Shu-chang and his friends left the Flying Crane.

Disappointed by how little he had learned, Shu-chang nevertheless was satisfied that he had made contact with He

Da. He suspected the man would prove to be a key to the victim's identity—and maybe his death.

The alley had darkened considerably since they'd entered the wine shop. The sun hid behind the two-story buildings lining the lane, refusing to brighten the congested neighborhood, and only adding to its dreary ambience.

"He had a feather in his cap," Shu-chang said.

"Many of the men in there did," Lin noted.

Zhou looked over at Lin and added, "Yeah, but He Da's their leader. I'm sure."

Lin and Fang nodded.

"He knows a lot more than he's saying," Shu-chang said. "And he essentially told the others not to talk to us." To keep frustration from building up, he turned to his companions. "We need to visit as many businesses and homes in this area as possible. Let's split up and go door-to-door with questions. Ask if anyone is missing from their family or from the neighborhood."

The three men agreed and, after quickly dividing up the blocks, they disbanded. Shu-chang had only covered one block when people started giving him wide berth as they passed. They avoided looking at him, but their eyes flicked to a spot behind him. A tingle crawled up his neck and the back of his head. He refused to look behind; to do so might make him appear afraid. Even so, his shoulders stiffened as he struggled to maintain an even pace.

It wasn't long before a burly fellow and a tautly muscled man overtook him, one on each side. The narrow alley forced them to touch his shoulders as they drew even. They slowed their steps to match his.

Shu-chang fought to control his breathing, even as his heart raced.

"Don't you know it's dangerous to be nosey?" the larger man whispered in a hoarse voice.

Shu-chang kept walking, neither slowing down nor speeding up. "Did you have something you wanted to tell me?" he asked, glancing at the stranger.

"Just that you should be careful. You never know who might want to hurt you," the fellow said, raising his eyebrows.

The threat suggested that Shu-chang knew more than he did. That he might have discovered something important. He held the man's gaze. "I'm only trying to find out the identity of the man who died. You know his ghost won't rest until I do," he added pointedly.

The thug shot a look of concern to his companion on the other side of Shu-chang. But he quickly recovered. "It's the living you have to worry about, not the dead." He smirked, then added, "You'd do best to leave the matter alone and not meddle." He stopped short and Shu-chang almost collided with the smaller fellow who had stepped in front, blocking his way.

Shu-chang looked from one to the other. The thugs had slipped into the stance of street fighters. He quickly glanced around them. The alleyway was no longer crowded and the few people walking past studiously avoided glancing in their direction. No one would come to his aid if these thugs beat him up.

As he assessed what he could do, a cheerful voice called out from the other side of the alley.

"Hey, Teacher."

A sense of relief rushed through him as Shu-chang gladly turned toward the man who was fast closing in on them. Zhou.

"Remember what I said. And forget nosing around," the thug growled into his ear. With that, the two intruders spun on their heels and hurried away.

Coming up to Shu-chang, Zhou grinned. "Looked to me

like you had unwelcome company. Thought you might like a little distraction."

Shu-chang couldn't hide his relief. "I believe you came just in time. A few seconds later and I could have been in trouble." He watched the two disappear down the lane, then turned back to his friend. "Any luck?"

"Not so far." He also looked at the retreating figures. "It may be best to come again tomorrow, in the morning. We could talk to the residents in twos, not individually."

"Hmm. Working in pairs might alleviate future problems. I hope."

"I live here. Let me accompany you out onto the main street. It'll be safer. No sense in giving anyone else an opportunity to mess with you."

Shu-chang nodded. "Glad to have your company. But I can't interview tomorrow morning. Classes. Come to the school in the early afternoon and we can start then."

Shu-chang strolled back to Uncle Xin's. Although his mind was engaged in turning over the scant information he had gleaned at the Flying Crane, he remained vigilantly aware of his surroundings.

People milling around him on the street appeared innocent, but were they? Was anyone watching him? Was he overreacting?

Just as he began to doubt his senses, he spotted the two men who'd stopped him earlier following him at a slight distance. This time, however, they didn't approach him.

Shu-chang didn't want to get into a fight. He knew his limitations. He shifted his robe and flapped out his sleeves.

A vendor raised a call, praising the pork-filled buns he was selling. Shu-chang stopped, bought one, and nibbled on it while chatting with the peddler about the weather. As he did so, he kept a careful eye on the two men. They paused at another food cart along the road.

His heart constricted. Not good. He forced his newly tensed muscles to relax. Moving along at a leisurely pace, he turned at the next intersection and swiftly side-stepped into a modest leather store.

"Ah, Teacher Shu-chang! Good to see you," the merchant said.

"Sir. I need to ask a favor," Shu-chang said, grateful to be recognized. "Could I exit through your back area?"

The merchant threw him a curious glance. Going out the back door meant passing into the man's private living quarters. Nevertheless, without further comment, he agreed. "Come this way."

An advantage of being a local teacher, Shu-chang thought. After quickly checking to make sure no one was entering the store, he gratefully followed the shop owner's lead.

Just as Shu-chang exited the building, he heard the shop owner loudly greet new customers. A familiarly deep, male voice responded.

Shu-chang hurried down the alley and, after taking a couple more jogs at crossroads, left the warren behind. He lost no time getting to his classroom, where he collapsed into a chair.

CHAPTER 12

The *shir-shir* of Xiang-hua's felt-soled shoes softly announced her movements down the veranda. Reaching the classroom, she halted and peered around the doorway. Shu-chang sat at his desk, cradling his head in his hands. He looked exhausted and out of sorts.

Her brow wrinkled. "How are you? You're quite flushed and breathing hard. What happened?"

He jumped at the sound of her voice.

She paused before stepping inside. Was he embarrassed at her seeing him this way? She didn't mean to intrude.

"I'm fine. Too much hurrying around," he said and dropped his hands to the desk. "Come in, come in."

Xiang-hua had been waiting on the veranda, hoping to see Shu-chang on his return. She'd wanted to share her morning's finds, and she was eager to learn what he'd discovered as well. While her job as coroner was finished, she couldn't let the case go. It'd help to discuss it with him. Her desire in talking with him wasn't personal, she told herself, strictly professional. After all, they had worked well together before.

She slipped into the room and sat in a chair opposite him.

"Seeing that stranger's mutilated body must have been quite a shock," Shu-chang said. "I'm sorry you had to be involved."

"It was my duty," she said, maintaining her composure while pushing away unbidden images elicited by his words. She didn't want him to think she was weak.

As if sensing her discomfort, Shu-chang quickly added: "It was disturbing to me too. To everyone."

Xiang-hua paused to steady herself. To distract from the images roiling around in her mind, she reached into her sleeve, retrieved a small sack, and pulled out a folded object.

"I found something before I left the herbalist's pigsty."

Shu-chang cocked his head and asked the obvious: "You didn't give what you found to Zhong?"

"I didn't have a chance. I haven't even told father yet. When Lady Jiang's servant came for me, all of my attention went to what I needed to do for her. I had to prepare my medicine kit, but I didn't know what to bring." *Oh, I'm rambling. Now he'll think I'm flighty*, she thought, dismayed. "And, as I've just returned home, and father is still out on business, I thought I'd stop by ... here." She looked around as if to find a reason to be there.

"I'm glad you came," Shu-chang said. "We can compare what we've both discovered. That should give us a good start."

Xiang-hua nodded, happy at his unquestioning complicity in searching for the murderer.

"I found this," she said, laying a small, ragged cloth down between them and smoothing it out. "It's a torn piece of blue cloth that was snagged on the top of the pen's enclosure. It may be important. Or not."

Shu-chang leaned forward, eyes bright.

"We can't be certain about when it was snared in the wall, but it couldn't have been too long ago. It sprinkled yesterday, and the cloth hasn't been rained on."

He examined the fragment, then replaced it on the table. "The dead man's clothing didn't have such a hole," Shu-chang said.

"It could belong to Shi. It's his pigsty. But, if it isn't—"

"There's a reasonable chance it belongs to our mystery perpetrator," Shu-chang finished.

She nodded. "I also found a line of grain." She reached into her sleeve and pulled out the packet she'd stuffed into it this morning. She laid it out on the table and opened it. "How it fits in with the death is unclear. But here it is." Her brow furrowed in concentration.

Shu-chang poked a finger into the grain, pushing the seeds around. "It's not rice. Some kind of grass?"

"That would be my guess."

"Right. Yet hard to see how it could be related to anything."

"For now, anyhow," Xiang-hua said. She agreed, but even the most inconsequential detail could be enlightening. She would not disregard the little golden grains.

Shu-chang shrugged his shoulders. Then, pointing to the blue cloth, he said: "That's interesting but may not tell us much, either. A good many of the laborers wear trousers made of that blue material."

"Yes, but only one will have a torn area that matches this patch. The problem will be to find that person before he has a chance to repair the tear. Patched clothing is not exceptional either."

"And what about your medical findings?"

Xiang-hua gazed at the objects on the table. She slowly gathered them up, placed them in her bag, and dropped the bundle back into her sleeve. She considered how to answer him. Discussing the dead man was disturbing. She could admit that to herself. But she had to gather her strength, to create the professional distance necessary. At the same time, she didn't want Shu-chang to think she was uncaring or oblivious to the import of a man's death.

Hoping he'd recognize her concern and also her professionalism, she took a deep breath and proceeded.

"The victim had one significant deep cut in his back. From the look of the wound, it was probably made with a knife. I believe that's what killed him. The mutilation to his face happened after his death."

"What about signs of blood? I didn't see much."

She pursed her mouth in thought, then said, "I didn't either."

"Hmm," Shu-chang said. "Perhaps the murderer killed him elsewhere and dragged him to the pen."

"Yes, that is most likely. Unfortunately, the ground was so disturbed it was impossible to tell if he'd been stabbed there or elsewhere. If he had been killed in Shi's pen, I would normally expect a pool of blood somewhere on the ground. I could tell from the purple discoloration of the back of his body and legs that he'd been lying on his back for some time. Nevertheless, I didn't see significant signs of blood from the wound on the ground." Xiang-hua took a deep breath and released it. She hoped this was the last time she had to perform the job of a coroner. She much preferred helping the living.

"What about time of death?"

"Probably late night, very early morning. I can't say." She puckered her lips in thought. "It had to be when it was still dark. Who would carry a body through the streets at sunrise?"

He nodded. "I looked around the area, too. Eventually, I found drag marks between the pen and lane and followed them as best I could to Shou Road. You remember Zhou and his friends who helped us in the past, don't you? I ran into them in the warren and, it turns out, they were familiar with a gang hangout called the Flying Crane. Zhou thought it might give me a lead, so they took me over to the wine house, and I was able to scout it out." He paused for a breath.

"And? What did you find?"

Shu-chang frowned. "Not much. Nothing really. Except confirming that the White Feather Gang hangs out there. Given that feather found with the body, there is probably some connection. But at this point, I don't have anything concrete. I'll keep checking."

He tapped his chin repeatedly before continuing: "When I was at Shi's place, his neighbor, Yao-sheng, made a point of coming over and accusing Shi of the crime. He proffered no real evidence, just ranted on." He looked up at Xiang-hua. "What I don't understand is why he was so belligerent and insistent on arresting the herbalist. Falsely accusing someone is a serious breach of the law."

"Maybe his wife would be able to enlighten us. I noticed her when I was at the herbalist's this morning. The doorway's shadow concealed her, but she was there. Watching." Xiang-hua let her fingers rest on the table. "Besides telling us more about the hard feelings between her husband and Shi, she could have seen something. Their house is so close. Even their pigpens almost touch each other."

"I agree, but her husband would rightly be furious if I went to interview her," Shu-chang said, holding his hands up, palms out, as if to forbid his meeting her.

"Perhaps, if *you* talked to her," Xiang-hua agreed. "But ... I could stop by to make sure she's okay after such a terrible thing happened so close to their home. She might talk to me. Yao-sheng can't object to a doctor's visit to his wife."

He nodded, swallowing his objections. By all accounts,

and from the neighbor's earlier behavior, Ms. Chen's husband was an angry, violent man. Shu-chang stared at Xiang-hua. Torn between wanting to protect her and realizing that he really couldn't stop her from going, he nodded once more. Nevertheless, a prickle of fear crept up the back of his head.

CHAPTER 13

Xiang-hua's coat billowed behind her as she stepped outside her home's gate and onto the street. Instead of her medicine bag, she swung a lidded, woven basket in her right hand. Along with a small, wrapped package, the basket held a few pieces of fruit and a winter melon. Her visit to Ms. Chen wasn't only medical; it was also a visit from a concerned neighbor. These gifts would nourish the young wife's *qi* in this time of stress.

It was late afternoon, and there was every likelihood that Ms. Chen would be home alone while Yao-sheng tended his fields. As she passed the herbalist's pigpen and approached Yao-sheng's simple house with its pen, she was impressed by how alike the two residences were. Of course, that was to be expected. Most small farmers in the area had similar homes: single- or two-room dwellings set snugly on the road with an enclosed backyard connected to their fields by a dirt path. The yards were for the families' chickens and pigs, if they were lucky enough to have them. The fields were usually a short walk away, outside the town. The animals were kept close to the house to protect them and to easily collect their manure. Both human and animal wastes, used as fertilizer for the family crops, were considered as precious as gold. Nothing was discarded.

Careful not to let Yao-sheng's chickens out of his partially enclosed yard, Xiang-hua opened the gate and stepped through. She approached the house and exited through a second gate—once more making sure the chickens didn't follow. As she glanced toward the building, a shadowed form moved away from its only window.

On the ground to the door's right sat a bowl of rice and a burnt incense stick. Xiang-hua glanced at the traditional offering to wandering, malevolent ghosts—those whose deaths were ill-fated or who had no family to care for them. Such offerings were a common sight. She carefully stepped around the bowl, switched the basket to her left hand, and knocked. The door immediately swung open.

A sturdy young woman stood in the shaft of sunlight. Her unassuming dark pants and long, indigo over shirt, cinched at the waist, couldn't hide her solid, generous form. The material had been repaired several times; nevertheless—except for a few seeds clinging to her sleeve—her clothing was clean. Her ebony hair was pulled back and tied at the nape of her neck. She scowled, distorting what could be a pleasant face.

"Ms. Chen?" Xiang-hua inquired.

"Yes. May I help you?" The young woman's eyes danced between Xiang-hua and the space behind her.

"I'm Xin Xiang-hua, the local women's doctor. I was the coroner this morning, and since that unfortunate accident happened next door to you, I thought I'd stop by to make sure you're doing all right."

Ms. Chen's chin rose. "Why wouldn't I be? That had nothing to do with me." She rubbed the palm of her hand on her left hip as she held the door.

"Of course not. Forgive me if I seem too forward. I don't

mean to over-step my duties as a doctor." Xiang-hua ducked her head momentarily. "My grandmother isn't here to guide me. You may have heard of her. Grandma Xin?"

"Ah yes, even I know of your honorable grandmother." She relaxed a bit and looked past Xiang-hua again. "And, it's not that you're not welcome. It ... it's just that this terrible incident at our neighbor's has been trying. So many people standing around, staring. It's overwhelming. But I'm fine, really." She moved back into the darkened room.

"I brought you something. It's not much. Just something we had at home," Xiang-hua said, minimizing her gift while holding the basket up.

Ms. Chen's face relaxed and her eyes brightened. "Thank you, thank you. That's not necessary."

"Please. I'd be happy if you accepted it."

Ms. Chen allowed herself to be convinced and, taking the basket, invited Xiang-hua in.

Xiang-hua stepped over the threshold and entered the cramped, musty interior. She cast a quick glance around. The hard-packed dirt floor had been swept clean. A brick kang and two scarred stools filled the room's space. A shelf halfway up the opposite wall held a vase with spent incense sticks and an earthen cup. A well-used kettle rested on top of a stove built into one corner. Ms. Chen closed the door behind Xiang-hua, allowing a gloom to overpower the patch of light coming through the single window.

"Would you like hot water?" the young wife asked, moving over to the stove. She started bundling a small packet of sticks together, placed them in the stove's lower area, and lit it.

Water. Not tea. If there had been tea in the house, it would have been offered. Observing Yao-sheng's wife, Xiang-hua guessed her to be about her own age. And yet—she again glanced around the room—her life was so different. It wasn't just the palpable poverty of the surroundings; the bareness of the space bespoke a coldness, a lack of human warmth. Xiang-hua shivered.

While waiting for the water to boil, they sat together on the kang, legs folded beneath them. Ms. Chen fairly radiated anxiety. Her hands were in perpetual motion: patting her thighs, flying up to straighten her sleeves or her blouse's lapels, then down to her thighs, again.

"Are you from Jian?" Xiang-hua asked.

"My family lives in a village south of here. I came to Jian three years ago, when I married my husband."

Three years ago. That meant Ms. Chen had been about fourteen when she married. Xiang-hua peeked around. No sign of a child anywhere. Although she tried not to be too obvious in her perusing of the room, Ms. Chen noticed.

"We don't have any children. Yet," she said in a lowered voice. Her forehead furrowed into a frown.

"You're young. There's time."

Ms. Chen silently nodded. The light was too dim to be sure if the look Xiang-hua caught in her eyes indicated a troubled soul.

Ms. Chen jumped up and busied herself by pulling out two clay cups and filling them with hot water. She brought one over to Xiang-hua and, cradling it in two hands, placed it down on the kang in front of her. She went back for her own cup and returned with the basket. Sitting next to Xiang-hua, she opened it and took out a piece of fruit. She reached over to the stove, grabbed a small plate and knife, and started cutting the fruit into pieces. Placing each piece in a pleasing pattern on the plate, she offered it to Xiang-hua, who took one. Ms. Chen followed suit. When she bit into the fruit, a line of juice slipped down her chin. She giggled and swiped it away.

After munching on the treats and making small talk,

Xiang-hua asked: "You're normally up pretty early in the morning, aren't you?"

"I get up before dawn, start the fire, and make rice. My husband likes the room to be warm when he gets up."

"Did you see anything unusual last night or this morning?"

Ms. Chen shook her head. "Is that when the man died?"

"Yes."

"Was he murdered?"

"It looks like it."

The young wife shivered and looked out at Shi's walled enclosure. "How awful. That's bad for Master Shi." She shifted her gaze to the knife and plate sitting near them. "Finding the dead man on his property, I mean."

Xiang-hua was here to gather information, not share details about the death, so she said, "Yes, it doesn't look good for him. Although he claims the man could have been injured in a fight and accidentally fell into the pen as he passed by." She put the last of the food onto Ms. Chen's plate before continuing. "It's unclear right now. Did your husband say anything to you? About seeing or hearing someone?"

"No, but he was out last night."

"Was that unusual? Being gone all night?"

Dropping her head, Ms. Chen spoke more to the plate of fruit than to Xiang-hua: "He likes to gamble. He is often out."

"Not many wine shops stay open all night," Xiang-hua nudged.

"Oh, he only goes to the Flying Crane. He says it's the only wine house where the gamblers are honest." She gave a short laugh. "An honest gambler. Doesn't keep him from losing a lot of money," she said, not hiding the bitterness in her tone.

"When did he return home?"

"He came in early this morning, before sunrise. I was still

asleep. He woke me. Told me to get up and cook rice."

"Hmm. An earlier breakfast than usual?"

Ms. Chen shifted positions. "As soon as the rice was finished, he put a dish outside with the incense."

"Does he often do that? Feed the ghosts?" Many people put food, wine, and incense outside their door to appease the hungry ghosts who roamed the land. Hungry ghosts were the spirits of people who had died without heirs and had no one to rely on to care for them in the afterlife, where their needs —food, money, a home—were the same as in this life. If they were not fed and taken care of by the living, they became angry and, therefore, dangerous.

"That's the first time." She smirked. "He's always made fun of people for wasting food and drink in that way. 'Let a ghost try to cause trouble,' he'd say and laugh."

Xiang-hua sipped her water. Bold words indeed. "But now he's changed his mind."

Ms. Chen shrugged.

After a little more time, Xiang-hua prepared to leave. She rose and reached into her sleeve to remove a small bag of medicine. "Take this each night before you go to bed. It will help you sleep."

Ms. Chen declined the packet. "I have no money to pay you," she said simply.

"Don't worry about that. You have suffered a shock with this terrible event next door. This will help."

Finally, the young wife gratefully accepted the medicine.

At the door, Xiang-hua said, "I will come by again to see how you're doing." Turning away, she was again struck by how different their lives were. She had so many advantages—a strong family, a comfortable life, even an education. What had she done to deserve this? What had Ms. Chen done to warrant her present life? Was it luck? Was it karma? Was it fate?

While she left through the front door, Xiang-hua slipped along the side and returned to the footpath running behind the houses. She wanted to see the herbalist Shi's pigpen once more.

The corpse still lay on a board near the house. No one had come to claim the body. Who was that man, to have ended his life in such a horrific way and to have no one to claim or mourn him? Was his death due to bad karma or to the lifepath he'd chosen? Could they find his murderer and bring his spirit peace through justice?

These questions swirled around her as she slowly proceeded down the path, head down, lost in concentration.

"Good afternoon, Sister," a friendly voice called out.

Xiang-hua perked up. A tall, lanky woman stood in a minuscule yard with two chickens pecking at her feet. She waved broadly at Xiang-hua, then motioned for her to come closer.

Crossing over, Xiang-hua smiled at the woman. The young doctor had treated her daughter for a minor, but persistent, illness a few months ago. "How have you been? How is your daughter doing?"

"She's well." Then, giving herbalist Shi's and Ms. Chen's houses a significant look, she said, "I see you're involved with the incident over there." She paused, waiting, hoping, for Xiang-hua to fill her in on the details.

"I can only tell you what you probably already know. A stranger was found dead in the herbalist's pigpen. The head of village security, Zhong, and Teacher Shu-chang are investigating." Looking over her shoulder back toward Shi's, Xiang-hua noted how clear a view of the property this neighbor had. "Did you notice anything unusual last night or early this morning?"

"No. We go to bed soon after dark and I'm busy with cooking early in the morning." She wiped her nose. "I hardly know Gao Shi or Yao-sheng and his wife. They all keep to themselves. Friendly enough but keep to themselves," she repeated.

"Ah, I see. And they are close to each other?"

"All I know is that herbalist Shi goes to visit Yao-sheng's fairly often. People claim they have financial dealings. Of course, I know nothing about that," she said with a sniff.

"The fellow found in the pen had tattoos on his arm. Have you ever seen a man like that around here before?"

The woman scrunched her mouth in concentration. "Yes, I did see a fellow recently around the house. He was starting to repair the pen's front wall. See there?" She waved a hand toward a partially patched area. "He had a tattoo on his arm. I remember because when I saw it, I started to worry." She patted her chest. "Gang members wear tattoos. It's careless of Shi to hire criminals to work for him." She quickly shook her head in disapproval.

"Has he hired other gang members?" Xiang-hua asked.

"Once or twice before. Those tattoos were easy to see because they work shirtless. I keep my daughter inside the house where they can't see her." She shuffled from one foot to the other. "She's almost old enough to marry. Soon we'll find her a husband."

Xiang-hua didn't comment. The girl was thirteen. Marrying daughters off just before or soon after they reached menses was not unusual among poor peasant families. One fewer mouth to feed.

"Any idea what gang they belonged to?" Xiang-hua asked, turning attention back to the victim.

"That I can't say. I can tell you one thing, though. That herbalist acts like a friendly fellow, but you have to ask: What kind of man hires gang members to work for him? Even if it is for repairing his house and wall. You don't bring a snake into the house to clean out the mice."

CHAPTER 14

The next day, Shu-chang sat at his desk. The students had gone, and his classroom was quiet. He valued the little time he had in the afternoons to read and prepare for the third national examination. Passing in the top five percent would guarantee a position in the emperor's government, with the concomitant elite social status and economic prosperity. His father's dream for him would be achieved, and his family's name and honor would be assured.

Besides, passing the examination was something he knew he could accomplish if he studied and worked hard. After all, among all the candidates who took the second examination, he had placed at the highest level.

His eyes traced over the Confucian texts at his side. He only wished that he could also be successful in his other duty to his family: finding his father and uncle's murderers. So far, all lines of inquiry had led nowhere. He was at a loss as to what to do next. *Well*, he thought as he looked at the study materials before him, *at least I can do this*.

Today, however, he had no more than taken out his books

and paper when a servant came to announce that someone wished to see him.

"Who is it?"

"A local farmer. Says it's very important that he see you as soon as possible."

With a sigh, Shu-chang set down his book. "Bring him in."

The young teacher watched as a disheveled man with rolled sleeves followed the servant down the veranda. As the stranger passed the window, he nervously retied his jacket's belt and straightened his hat. Entering the room, he bowed deeply.

"I am Gao Huai-liang. I have a small house and field near herbalist Shi's. I have come here ... that is, I have come to request that you write a petition for me. One to be filed in court. At the magistrate's yamen."

Shu-chang cocked his head and studied the newcomer closely. He was wiry and obviously strong. "Why don't you ask one of the scribes on the street? There are plenty in front of the yamen."

Huai-liang dropped his gaze to the floor in front of Shu-chang. "I ... I can't afford to travel to the provincial capital to have one of those scribes do this. If you write it out, I can have the petition delivered for me."

Shu-chang pursed his lips and nodded. "You realize that petitioning the court is a very serious affair."

"I've thought about it. I must do this." His voice dropped to little more than a whisper. "I have no choice."

"What's so important that you feel you need to take such drastic action?" Shu-chang asked. He had to be direct because once the wheels of justice started moving, the innocent as well as the guilty could get crushed beneath their unstoppable progression. He wanted to make sure Huai-liang understood this. Although, truth be told, he'd be surprised that any grown man would not be aware of this immutable fact.

The farmer nervously rubbed his hands together. Finally, he said: "I have bad karma. My whole life ... I've always had bad fate. I must do this now ... to prevent that demon Shi blaming me for something I didn't do."

Shu-chang remained silent. His silence encouraged the visitor to continue.

"I have a farm next to Shi's. He's a terrible neighbor, always complaining about this or that ... accusing me or my animals of causing problems."

"Does he have reason to blame you or your animals?"

Huai-liang pulled himself up to his full height. "No. I am a small farmer. I work hard. I never cause problems. He lies."

"What is it you want me to write? What is the problem?"

Huai-liang wordlessly rubbed his hands together. "Last week, my water buffalo accidentally strayed onto his land. It died that night ... poisoned," he said haltingly. Then, corralling his anger, he quickly added, "He owes me a water buffalo."

"Had your water buffalo been sick before he strayed off your land?"

"He wasn't sick. He was strong. Healthy. Now he's dead. It's Shi's fault and he won't pay up."

"You believe Shi should pay you even though you now admit that your water buffalo ate his crop?"

"He grows many of his herbs on a piece of his farm. I don't know what they are but I'm sure many of them are poisonous. Dangerous. He should grow them only in a ... in a safe place ... within his walled courtyard. Not out in an open field."

Clearly this was a murky problem. One best settled the traditional way: by the local, elder members of the town's elite. They knew the people involved and would keep the incident from causing other, bigger, problems for all concerned. Shu-chang leaned away from the farmer. "You should take your complaint to the town's elders. They will settle this."

"Shi is their friend. They will side with him against me. It would be useless to go to them," Huai-liang said.

"Why are you just now wanting to write a petition to the court? It's been a week."

Huai-liang rubbed his hands together more vigorously; his gaze never left the floor. "I was afraid."

"Afraid? Of what?"

"The court."

"So, what changed your mind? Why now? Is there something else you need to tell me before I agree to write this petition for you?"

The farmer didn't respond.

Shu-chang waited.

"Shi might accuse me of killing that man to frame me."

Shu-chang stared at the sorrowful figure in front of him. Where did this come from? It was quite a leap. "Why would he do that?"

"To get out of paying for my water buffalo."

Shu-chang shook his head. "There's more to this than what you've told me so far. I can't help you if I don't know the full story. Why in the world would he blame you for the death of a man you didn't know?"

"I knew him," Huai-liang said in a barely audible voice.

Shu-chang leaned forward but said nothing.

"The dead man. I knew him. I've seen him at the wine shop I go to ... sometimes go to."

"And," Shu-chang said to encourage more.

Huai-liang sighed deeply and dropped his hands to his side. "I'm afraid Shi will accuse me of killing him because Shi wants to avoid paying for my buffalo and he wants my land. If I'm executed for murder, he not only doesn't have to pay for my animal, he could also get my farm to add to his." Looking up at Shu-chang, his eyes flashed. "That herbalist is an evil man."

Shu-chang settled back against the chair once more. A buffalo was an expensive animal, but was it worth lying to the courts? If Shi falsely accused Huai-liang of a murder and the court found out, Shi would be executed for his deception. Shu-chang's head spun. He'd have to get the proper forms for submitting such an accusation, which he'd never done before. Even more critical, if he wrote the legal document for Huai-liang, what would be his own culpability? He passed his hand over his eyes. If he refused to help, the poor man may not have any other access to justice.

"Getting the court's official forms will take a couple of days. I will let you know when I have them, and then we can write up your petition."

The farmer perked up. "Thank you, sir," he said enthusiastically, again bowing deeply. "Thank you."

Once alone, the farmer's words slipped in and out of Shu-chang's mind. He sat back. What had Huai-liang suggested? That the murder could have arisen out of spite? But not against the dead man. It all sounded rather convoluted to him: that Shi was willing to kill a third party in order to frame the farmer, entangling him in a downward spiral of court costs and possible criminal liability. It didn't make sense on the face of it. Especially given where the body was found.

Shu-chang studied the empty door of his classroom. Of course, if Huai-liang were accused and circumstantial evidence existed, he could be found guilty. In that case, he would be executed. But even if found innocent, he could still be bankrupted and lose all his property in defending himself. He very likely would even be tortured in an attempt to get at the truth.

On the other hand, if Shi had no such intention in mind—and was completely innocent himself of any involvement in the murder—Huai-liang's pro-active move to bring a case against him could seriously backfire. Was the illiterate farmer aware that torture was an acceptable legal technique used by the court to force the guilty, and the innocent, to tell the truth?

As Shu-chang chewed over this new problem, Xiao-ren barged into the room. Seeing his cousin at the desk, book in hand, the boy halted abruptly. His furrowed brow and tense mouth relaxed. A gleeful smile spread across his face.

"Teacher! I heard about those thugs threatening you yesterday. I'm happy to see that you're not hurt."

Upon seeing the boy's obvious expressions of concern and relief, Shu-chang refrained from chastising him for his rambunctious demeanor. However, he couldn't help but remind his student of his primary duties. "You missed class again today. And why aren't you in your room studying?"

Xiao-ren flinched, but only slightly. "I was about to do that. Something came up." Before Shu-chang could reprimand him for not doing what he was told, Xiao-ren hurriedly continued, "I was able to learn something about the herbalist that might interest you."

"And what might that be?"

"That Yao-sheng, the guy who lives next door to Shi, is furious with him and bragged that he would destroy him. He said the herbalist would be sorry he ever crossed him."

Shu-chang leaned forward. "What was Yao-sheng so angry about? What had Shi done?"

Xiao-ren frowned. "I don't know. Only that he was really, really angry."

"Why would Yao-sheng be out and about telling people that he wants to destroy Shi?"

"He was at the wine house and drunk. The guys said that he drinks a lot, and when he does he gets belligerent and rants."

"Ranting is just talk. It probably means nothing," Shu-chang said, disappointed. Drunkenness and angry, careless talk often went together. A way of letting off steam without being taken seriously.

Xiao-ren's shoulders dropped.

"Where did you hear all of this, anyway? Where were you?"

The boy's eyes slid to the side. "At a small tea shop on Shou Road."

"Tea shop?" Shu-chang repeated, staring at his cousin.

"They do serve tea," he said, shifting from foot to foot.

Shu-chang wanted to explode. Xiao-ren always seemed to walk a fine line between being obedient and breaking all the rules. He took a deep breath and asked, "Did he say what he intended to do to Shi?"

"Not directly, no. But the guys thought dumping a dead body in his pigpen could bring disaster on Shi's head. Even without a conviction, he'd be ruined. Who would trust an herbalist tainted with the brush of murder?"

Shu-chang nodded. "Of course, that still leaves open the question of why that particular man was killed. Could he have been involved with both Shi and Yao-sheng?"

"I didn't hear anything about the dead fellow." Xiao-ren's face dropped at his admission.

"Hmm. If we didn't have a body, it'd be as if the victim never existed. Someone must have known him or seen him before." Pushing his papers aside, he stood up. "You did a good job but now you must go to your room and study."

Xiao-ren pouted. "I—"

"I have to go now, myself. Do as I say."

Sulking, Xiao-ren left the room. Shu-chang watched him turn down the veranda toward his room. He flexed his shoulders and prepared to leave. It was time to meet Zhou, Fang, and Lin.

CHAPTER 15

Xiang-hua prepared to visit Lady Jiang's mother-in-law first thing in the morning. She opened the door to a tidy work space, revealing her grandmother's, and now her, lab. Vessels of various sizes lined the shelves; baskets of fresh and dried plants clustered together on a side table; large ceramic jars with marinating tinctures stood against the wall. As she entered the room, she inhaled the unique aroma that never failed to lift her spirits. The cool, damp morning air carried the medicinal odors of the many herbs and tinctures —whether fragrant, pungent, or acrid—and mixed them together as one.

Xiang-hua rechecked the medicinal package she'd orga- nized for Lady Jiang last night. Besides following a strict food regime, she wanted the older woman to begin taking the medicine as soon as possible. She slipped it into her medicine bag and left.

Upon Xiang-hua's arrival, the elderly maid once again led her directly into Lady Jiang's quarters. Lady Jiang joined her moments later.

"My mother-in-law is already doing better," she said, smiling. "She slept well and is actually eating some of her break-fast this morning, thanks to you."

The news more than delighted Xiang-hua. Her improve-ment was affirmation that Xiang-hua had diagnosed her problem successfully. She reached into her bag and pulled out the satchel she'd prepared earlier. "I have another herbal mixture I want you to give her. You'll prepare it as a tonic and she can drink it as a warm tea."

She handed it over to Lady Jiang, who took it rather reluc-tantly. "Do you think she'll need this? She's doing so much better already."

"It's good that she's showing improvement," Xiang-hua said, "but her condition requires careful and steady support, or she'll slip back into her disharmony. This is especially true of the elderly. Her constitution is no longer as robust as it once was."

Lady Jiang nodded. She ordered the maid to bring a pot of hot water to her mother-in-law's room. Once the maid left, she led Xiang-hua into the adjoining room. The air was as stultifying as yesterday, but the matriarch now sat up in one of two chairs at a small, simple, ebony table. A few dishes were scattered over its top. A scrambled egg floated in a bowl of broth. Another bowl held a finely sliced cooked squash, and the third was a bowl of plain rice.

At their entering the room, the older woman looked over and smiled in greeting. "Come. Sit." She motioned to Xiang-hua. Then, turning to her daughter-in-law, she said, "Prepare tea for our visitor."

Although she knew the maid would be bringing in hot water shortly, Lady Jiang nodded and left the room.

"It's good to see you again so soon. But, as you can see, I'm doing better already. Thanks to you." She proffered a sunny smile. "I'm sure I won't be any trouble anymore. So, what brings you here this morning? Surely Fen-peng didn't ask for you to come."

"No, no. Fen-peng hasn't requested that I return." Xiang-hua looked over her patient. "I'm glad to see how well and how quickly you've responded to the medicine. However, that was the first step in raising your qi and building you back up. To continue your progress, I brought another herbal mixture to balance your qi."

"This old lady is causing you too much trouble," the elderly woman said, shaking her head.

"Please, continue with your breakfast. I am not a guest. I am your doctor and eating is a part of your getting well." She looked over the dishes. "Meat is especially important."

The old woman nodded somberly. "My daughter-in-law takes good care of me." Her hand fluttered over the dishes on the table. "I have plenty to eat, while she eats very little."

"You are the matriarch. She wants to care for you."

"She tries her best. Yesterday she bought a bit of pork. I couldn't chew it, so she softened it up by chewing it for me. She fed me pork and took none for herself. While not a vegetarian, she only eats grains." The Old Madam glanced away. "Meat is expensive."

"Hmm," Xiang-hua murmured. "Things will be better now that your son is home."

"Would it were so. He was gone a long time and my daughter-in-law had to carry the burden of keeping the house and watching my health. I am sad to say that instead of appreciating all that she's done, Fen-peng has developed an unreasonable jealousy toward that herbalist she's been buying my medicines from."

This was the second time Xiang-hua had heard about Fen-peng's jealousy. Only now it was from his mother. How serious of a problem was it? The gossips claimed that this household—his responsibility—also suffered economically. Having just the gatekeeper and the old maid as servants certainly indicated hard times, and also meant that Lady Jiang had to have significantly more contact with the world outside the traditional women's quarters. There was no male relative or appropriate servant to intervene for her.

"Still, Fen-peng's being home will lighten her burden," Xiang-hua said to sooth the older woman, who was becoming agitated.

"I hate to say it, but, although my son is not a violent man, he does have a few weaknesses. Weaknesses that many men have."

"Hmm," Xiang-hua murmured again.

The old woman shook her head. "He returned from his business trip with very little to show for all the time he was gone. And he's already started to spend significant time in the flower houses drinking and gambling. And, on top of that, he's jealous of his wife for doing what she had to do in his absence." She sighed, leaned back in her chair, and passed a trembling hand over her face.

Xiang-hua's heart went out to her patient. Throughout her training, she'd learned over and over again how necessary it was to achieve a balance in both one's body and one's life. It was clear to her that this was a household out of balance, but she was at a loss as to how she could help. She was only a doctor. What could she do? What should she do?

"My son is clever. We all thought he would pass the national examinations and achieve greatness for our family and the town. The world looked bright when he was young and Lady Jiang first came to our house as a new wife. But none of that was to be. Instead of studying, he frittered away his talent." She paused and looked away. "Perhaps that was my fault. I was too easy on him as a child. Not strict enough."

She coughed and shook her head. "While popular at parties because of his wit and elegant poetry, he never successfully passed even the first level examination. Although he did try. Several times." She sighed. "Having failed at that, he's become a merchant. Unfortunately, he's not proven to be a competent businessman either and has lost more than he made."

Xiang-hua glanced around the neat, time-worn room. How were they managing to pay the bills?

Before the older woman could say more, Lady Jiang returned with a tea tray and a kettle of hot water for the medicine. Xiang-hua moved the morning dishes aside as Lady Jiang brought the tray over. It slipped forward on the table and landed awkwardly on the burnished wood surface. The cups crashed noisily together and against the tea pot.

"Oh. I'm so clumsy!" Lady Jiang apologized as she began to collapse onto a nearby stool.

Xiang-hua pushed her chair back and jumped up to steady her. Helping Lady Jiang to the chair she had just abandoned, she said: "Please, sit here." Looking down at Lady Jiang's leg she asked: "What's bothering you? Did you hurt your leg?"

"It's nothing. I'm fine." She spread a protective hand over her right thigh.

"No, she's not," her mother-in-law protested. "She made a special medicinal broth for me two days ago and I'm afraid her leg is not recovering."

Xiang-hua glanced from one woman to the other, perplexed. "What does the broth have to do with your leg?" she asked Lady Jiang.

"She made a medicinal broth using her own flesh to nurture me and to make me strong." She straightened up from her slumped position and beamed at Lady Jiang. "My daughter-in-law is the most filial of women."

"You are too polite, mother," Lady Jiang demurred with an embarrassed tuck of her head.

It was all Xiang-hua could do to hold back a reprimand. They were talking about *gegu*, an old notion of caring for one's sick parents by feeding them your own flesh. It was rarely practiced anymore. Modern doctors like her grandmother did not believe in its use. It was against the Confucian axiom that a filial child would never desecrate her body in any way. Nevertheless, her grandmother also told her stories about people who continued to strongly believe that gegu was among the greatest of filial acts. Xiang-hua stared at Lady Jiang's right leg.

"You cut a piece of flesh from your leg," she said. It wasn't a question.

Lady Jiang looked down at her quivering hand resting on her thigh. "I must not be worthy enough. Mother is still ill. The medicine didn't work." She gently tapped her leg.

"All medicine takes time. It may be laying the foundation for what we are doing now," Xiang-hua gently exaggerated beyond what she believed herself. There was no sense in adding to the woman's anxiety and frustration. She didn't want to alienate Lady Jiang by challenging her beliefs. That wasn't her mission.

Putting aside her own annoyance at such an act, Xiang-hua insisted on checking Lady Jiang's temperature and reading her pulse. "Your qi is out of balance. Let me see your leg. I'll be able to make a paste to cure the infection."

Lady Jiang drew back. "It's not necessary. I am fine, really. I feel better already today. Old Madam worries unnecessarily about me."

"Curing the infection won't change the potency of your medicine. That's already been set," Xiang-hua said.

Turning slightly away from Xiang-hua, Lady Jiang said, "I am fine. Just a little weakness, that's all."

"Let her help," her mother-in-law pleaded.

"Mother, it's nothing, I assure you."

There was nothing Old Madam and Xiang-hua could say to convince Lady Jiang to accept an examination of her leg or any medicine. Exasperated, and doubting her own abilities as a doctor, Xiang-hua finally left, assuring them that she would be back again to check on Old Madam.

The gate flew open as she approached. Fen-peng strode through and into the courtyard, slamming the door closed behind him. Xiang-hua stepped back just as he was about to run into her. He halted abruptly.

"Ah, Sister. My apologies. I didn't expect anyone to be in my courtyard and didn't see you standing there. I'm afraid my mind was on other things."

"Master Xin Fen-peng," she said, stepping back.

Fen-peng scanned the space behind her as if seeking information. "I'm pleased that you were able to come so quickly to attend to my mother. She appears to be doing better under your care already."

"I've just been in to see her, and, yes, she is doing better, much better."

Fen-peng slapped his fist into his hand. "I don't know why my wife didn't call on you in the first place. Instead of that con man, Shi."

"It is natural to first seek remedies from an herbalist," Xiang-hua said. While true, she felt compelled to point out the obvious because he seemed incensed at Lady Jiang's decision.

"Perhaps." He shook his head. "My wife is a good, filial woman, but naive. She can be easily taken advantage of. Led astray." He abruptly turned to his old servant standing at the entrance. "Open the gate for Sister Xiang-hua." With a nod to Xiang-hua he added, "Thank you for coming. As I said,

I'm glad my mother is now under your care." Giving her a short bow, he stomped towards the house.

Xiang-hua watched him leave. Where had the fun-loving, witty man she'd heard about gone, leaving behind this unhappy, angry shell?

CHAPTER 16

Shu-chang dismissed Xiao-ren and, with the dead man's amulet tucked into his
voluminous sleeve, immediately left the classroom. Zhao and his friends milled around the street, just outside the small courtyard.

"We need to talk to a Taoist peddling his talents near the City God's temple," Shu-chang said as he joined them. "Yan-du suggested visiting a priest who sells amulets in front of the temple."

Without a word, the others fell in line beside him. The way became increasingly crowded as they moved further into the center of town. Peddlers and vendors with carts large and small sold foods and other goods while customers stood or sat on stools in the street eating their lunches.

A pair of men, wearing knee-length robes casually belted below their round stomachs, approached. The taller peddler held a tray stacked-to-overflowing with steamed buns and other street foods, cups, tiny sauce dishes, and a pot for pouring sauce. His partner smiled wide, wiped his hands on a long hand towel thrown over his shoulder, and cheerfully called out to them.

"Come! Eat! Enjoy the best of Jian!"

He beckoned to them with a pair of chopsticks pulled from his apron and waved toward the tray held by his friend.

Shu-chang declined, and they continued to move down the road, avoiding people clustered around food carts and scooping rice into their mouths or nibbling on steamed buns filled with red bean paste or a juicy pork mixture. Tiny restaurants lined the street on either side of the temple. Their small, round tables full of satisfied patrons.

In amongst the lunch-time crowd, a man wearing a black Taoist robe embroidered with gold I-Ching symbols sat hunched over a table. His body radiated deep concentration. In front of him, a woman stood anxiously gripping her hands, watching him intently.

Shu-chang paused. Zhou and the others stood behind him, waiting.

The Taoist priest's brush slowly and deliberately moved down a vertical strip of rice paper as he wrote out a series of characters. Laying his brush down on a shallow dish, he held the paper before him and offered up a prayer. Placing it back on the table, he took three large seals and, with the same deliberation, carefully pressed each stamp onto the strip.

Finally, he folded the paper several times, ending in a triangular self-enclosed packet. He handed the blessed talisman over to the woman. She immediately doubled over in a bow and reached out with two hands to accept it from him. Her pinched face softened and, clutching the packet before her, she bowed several times before tucking the treasure into her sleeve. After one more bow, she turned and disappeared into the crowded street.

Shu-chang indicated to Zhou and the men to remain

where they were, then he approached the table. "Sir, may we talk?"

The Taoist gazed at him for a moment, pulling on a single, long hair growing out of a mole on his chin. "What do you need?"

"I found this talisman and wonder if you could help me." Shu-chang pulled the paper out of his sleeve and offered it to the priest, who unraveled it. "Do you recognize it?"

The Taoist pursed his lips. "Yes, of course. It's a protection Fu."

"A protection Fu?" Shu-chang stared down at the muddied strip.

"Protection from evil. Or evil magic. The person who had this felt he needed a shield against something bad." He turned it over in his ink-stained fingers, gently touching the muddied areas. He couldn't hide the displeasure at seeing the Fu having been so disrespected.

"Do you know who could have written it?"

He turned the paper over in his hands again before nodding. "It's one of mine." He laid it on the table, gently smoothing it out as he did so.

"Do you remember who you wrote it for?"

His fingers again sought the single hair on his chin; he absently pulled it through his fingers. Then, tapping the paper, he said: "This type of talisman is not unusual. I do many. People come to me seeking solutions to their problems." He shrugged.

"But this is protection against evil magic. Would many people have need for that?"

"As I said, evil or evil magic. Bad spirits who disrupt their lives with sickness, extreme poverty. In today's world, many people need help." He looked up at Shu-chang. "Where did you get this?"

"It was found on the dead man in herbalist Shi's pigsty."

"Ah, yes. Evil, indeed. The power of the talisman could not overcome the man's karma." He picked the paper up and examined it more closely. "This one was written not long ago. It's from my current supply of paper. I started using it just this past month."

"The man was young, a little shorter than me, and had a large tattoo on his arm. Do you remember anyone like that coming by?"

The Taoist paused, staring at the paper. He shook his head. "Many, many need such a talisman. There were a couple of strangers; herbalist Shi; that farmer, Huai-liang ... That's all I remember."

"Huai-liang? You're sure?"

"Yes. It was for his wife. She was pregnant and very ill. Unfortunately, she couldn't change her karma either. She died after giving birth." As if answering Shu-chang's unasked question, he said, "A talisman can guide a person, support them in their behavior to improve their lot, but it can't completely alter their destiny. One's fate in this life is a result of past behavior, whether good or bad. What is pre-ordained is pre-ordained."

"Do you remember anything about those strangers? What they looked like? Anything they said that could help identify them?"

"No, not really." He paused again. "I don't know if it's of any use, but as they stood waiting for me to finish with another supplicant, I heard them mention the Flying Crane."

Well, that's something, Shu-chang thought as he turned to leave. Zhao and his men followed close behind. After stepping away from the Taoist, Zhao asked: "Should we pay another visit to the Flying Crane?"

"No. Not yet. We should check with others in the neighborhood first. The longer we wait, the less chance we have of getting someone to tell us what they saw or heard. I'm afraid we've already lost too much time. Undoubtedly, He Da's unenthusiastic reaction to our questioning is already all over the area."

"Yeah. It may very likely dampen the chances of anyone opening up to us. His influence runs way beyond the gang members," Zhou said. Li and Fang grunted their agreement.

"He's one mean fellow," Li said. "It'd take a brave, or foolish, man to cross him."

As they strolled down the street, a family of worshippers exited the City God's temple, cutting across their path. The four men stopped to let them pass. The sweet fragrance of incense wafted over the area as the family moved past.

The woodsy aroma pulled Shu-chang back to his father's funeral. His heart constricted. Enough time had passed that he no longer had to wear the full mourning robe of rough, undyed cotton required at the death of one's father. Only the small bit of white cloth attached to his robe indicated he was still in mourning. But the pain of his loss and the need to find justice for his father and uncle were as immense as ever.

The weight of that duty bore down on him every waking moment. He often wondered if he had strayed from the path of filial piety, either by looking out for his own comfort and taking a job as teacher in a town away from his home village or by taking time, as he was now, to search for a stranger's murderer, rather than for the killers of his own father and uncle.

He paused and looked through the temple's gate of massive, time-worn logs supporting a sweeping, tiled roof. Although much grander than the temple in his village, it nevertheless provided him with the same familiar sense of comfort as the one at home.

Should he enter? Besides being the City God's residence, other important deities were present. An altar was dedicated to Guan Yu, the guardian of justice and promoter of morality, loyalty, and righteousness. And a third altar honored Tu-di Gong, the Earth God, whose duty was to protect people and whose responsibility was to report on what happened in his assigned district. Shu-chang could use their assistance in this case.

"Teacher, good to see you," a voice pulled him out of his momentary reverie.

He looked up as a young man exited the immense temple gate and closed in on him.

"Huai-liang," Shu-chang greeted the farmer, casting a glance at the dimmed temple's smoky interior from which he'd just exited. "Paying a visit to the gods?"

"Yes." He drew himself up. "I just finished petitioning the City God in my case against that herbalist Shi."

This news caught Shu-chang by surprise. Without a word, he raised his eyebrows and cocked his head.

The farmer waved a rough, calloused hand toward a shadowy figure receding within the temple proper. "I went to the monk to help me beg the City God for help. To protect me from whatever false accusations the herbalist might make against me. And to bring the full weight of justice down on the head of that evil man."

"I see," Shu-chang said, wondering if this was a pro-active move to make Huai-liang look more innocent or was, indeed, a sign of the man's innocence. It would be incredibly plucky if he wasn't innocent. Petitioning the City God for justice should only be done as a last resort. Would he dare do this simply as a ruse to throw off suspicion of his being the murderer? Shu-chang had a hard time believing this unassuming farmer could be that cynical and brazen.

"We just finished the indictment ceremony asking for divine intervention. It's simpler than the one for the provincial court. The monk needed the facts, that's all."

"What law are you accusing the herbalist of breaking?"

"The gods aren't concerned with our human laws. They are only concerned with the question of morality. Of proper behavior."

While his response was stiff and unnatural, his premise was unassailable. Shu-chang nodded. Laws were made by men, whereas the moral code was embedded in the cosmos and, therefore, superseded all human laws. By going to the City God the farmer wasn't side-stepping the emperor's system of justice. He was adding to it.

Shu-chang had been vaguely aware of the right of people to directly petition the gods for justice; however, he had never known anyone to actually do it. "What did the City God say or do about your indictment?" he asked.

"Nothing. At the moment. The monk cautioned me to be patient. It may take days for divine justice to take effect. The divine court has to do an investigation first." He slammed the back of his fist into his left hand as he said, "But there will be justice. Shi won't be able to deceive the celestial court so easily."

Shu-chang nodded. Yet, as with the earthly court system, involving the gods and seeking divine justice was not always as easy as it might appear. They had to consider not only the events as they are played out on earth, but also the past lives of the people involved, of their karma, all of which made divine retribution not as straightforward as a petitioner might hope.

If the gods or the provincial courts determined the herbalist Shi was innocent and Huai-liang had brought false charges against him, the young farmer had just opened the gateway to far more trouble than he currently feared.

Whether seeking imperial or celestial justice, getting entangled with any court system could create as many problems for the innocent as for the guilty. Both courts may be necessary in the pursuit of justice, but they were often best used as a last resort.

CHAPTER 17

The well-trodden footpath made walking as easy as taking the road and was much more inconspicuous. Xiang-hua swung a basket with a couple of pork-filled steamed buns and a bundle of medicines. She chose the buns because of their popularity as a delectable snack. She wanted to talk with Ms. Chen again, not only to make sure she was well, but also to find out more about the night the victim died. She was sure the young wife hadn't shared all that she knew.

Serene, empty farmhouses dotted the path. Most people were already out in the fields. A few were at the market selling their produce. A child's cry rose and then was gone, leaving only the soft buzzing of insects. Xiang-hua slowed as she passed the herbalist's and approached Ms. Chen's.

"Sister! Back so soon?"

Ms. Chen's gangly neighbor stood at her back gate. She scattered a handful of grain out for her chickens. They rapidly spread about the yard, pecking furiously at the bounty.

From her back yard, the nosy neighbor could clearly see both the Shi and Yao-sheng enclosed yards. The woman waved. Xiang-hua returned the greeting and joined the neighbor at the gate.

"After speaking with you last time, I remembered a bit more and thought you should know about it," the woman said, setting her grain basket on the short wall surrounding her. Nodding her head toward the houses across the path, she said, "I'm not one to gossip, but those two households were close. Very close." She paused. "Word is that Shi even lent Yao-sheng money. Often. And quite a bit." Smirking, she stared at Xiang-hua.

The doctor eyed her companion. What she was suggesting was different from what she had been willing to tell Xiang-hua earlier. Remembering her grandmother's admonition to use silence as a tool in gathering information, she merely nodded.

When Xiang-hua didn't respond, the woman went on. "The herbalist used to visit Yao-sheng's house often. When Yao-sheng was in his fields or away in town." She paused again.

As the import of her comment sunk in, a prickly heat moved up Xiang-hua's neck. "Are you saying Ms. Chen and Shi are in a relationship?"

"Not now, maybe. The traveling back and forth between houses stopped a couple of weeks ago. About the time that ruffian started working at Yao-sheng's."

"You're saying the dead man worked for Yao-sheng?" Xiang-hua blinked.

"Mm-hm. He was around, did some work on their roof. He was often here when Ms. Chen's husband was out, too." She nodded her head as if to accent a significant point.

"Are you suggesting Ms. Chen had affairs with these men?"

The woman putt-putted. "Just as bad. She can't hide what she's doing. This is what I've heard from the men in my house along with what I've seen with my own two eyes. Of course, normally I wouldn't say anything. But a man did die." She cast a glance around as if to be sure others would not overhear her.

"Why would a husband let another man take his wife? If anyone found out, it would be a serious crime," Xiang-hua asked innocently.

The woman looked Xiang-hua over. "You are so young. And protected. There is much in this world that you don't understand."

Xiang-hua's temper started to rise. How old did she have to be before everyone stopped acting like she was too young for this, too young for that? At least her grandmother trusted her and had faith in her abilities.

Controlling her irritation, she considered the possibilities. It would be incredible for Yao-sheng to allow non-relatives around his home when his wife was alone. Families too poor for their women to be secluded, nevertheless, tried to maintain a level of decorum involving the separation between their women and other men. For this kind of thing to go on, the husband, Yao-sheng, had to know. After all, many others already either suspected or knew about the illicit situation.

Xiang-hua said, "Still, what would cause Yao-sheng to do such a thing?"

"Ms. Chen's husband gambles. From what I hear, he gambles more than most. People say he's in debt to some pretty rough characters—gangsters—and has been for some time. From what I heard, he developed a way to make more money that worked for a while. But, then he lost it and needed even more money! I ask you: What does a poor farmer have to sell to cover such a debt?" She stopped to throw another handful of grain out for her chickens before nodding meaningfully toward Yao-sheng's house. "His wife's favors." She glared at Yao-sheng's closed gate.

Xiang-hua's initial embarrassment at Ms. Chen's possible affairs now turned to anger. How could a husband do such a thing? It was counter to all sense of family—not to mention the law.

"I thought you should know," the neighbor repeated. Her voice hardened. "Maybe the herbalist killed that ruffian."

"Why do you think that?" Xiang-hua asked.

"Because that new fellow was also benefiting from Ms. Chen's attention. Jealousy, obviously." She threw her head back. "Disgusting! The whole affair is disgusting and unnatural!"

Before Xiang-hua had a chance to react to the neighbor, all further conversation was halted by a bright voice calling out, "Morning!"

Xiang-hua looked over her shoulder at a middle-aged woman coming toward them. She wore baggy, dark blue pants and a jacket that fell just below her hips. She held a basket and swung it in time with her stride.

"Er-nu, you're late in attending your fields," the neighbor called out to the approaching woman, smiling.

"I had much work to do before I could leave the house," she said, stopping near them. She pressed a hand over her eyes before adding, "I'm so tired already, but my vegetables won't wait."

The neighbor turned to Xiang-hua. "Sister, this is Er-nu." She grinned at the newcomer. "Mother to our famous He Da."

Taken aback, Xiang-hua stared at the woman. He Da? She had heard that name before as she'd ministered to women within the warren. He had a reputation for being tough, maybe even dangerous.

"You're too kind," Er-nu said. She set the basket down and shook her hand to relieve the discomfort from carrying the heavy load.

"Well, he's done more than most around here. You're fortunate."

Er-nu nodded. "After losing three babies, I prayed to the goddess to give me one boy. Just one. I promised her I wouldn't eat meat for his entire childhood. Not until he reached a healthy manhood." She wagged her head from side to side. "She gave me He Da and I've kept my promise. I've not had one bite of meat since he was born."

"Ah," Xiang-hua said, as if remembering him. "Does he work at the Flying Crane?"

The woman shuffled back and forth. "Not for the Flying Crane, but he's usually there with his friends and boss. The wine house is where his boss handles all of his work."

"Smart businessman. Cheaper than having an office," the neighbor said.

"And the owner of the wine house doesn't mind?" Xiang-hua asked.

Er-nu shrugged her shoulders. "They drink and eat there. Why would he care?"

"And protect the place, too," the neighbor woman said with a knowing smirk.

"That too," Er-nu said. "Who would dare cause trouble with them there?"

The implied gang affiliation was not lost on Xiang-hua. Could she possibly get the name of the gang leader from He Da's mother? She had to try. Eyeing the basket, Xiang-hua said, "His work must keep him too busy to tend to the fields"

"He's always working. He makes more than our little plot can provide. Besides," she chuckled self-depreciatingly, "I can still tend the farm. It's not easy and my back often complains, but I can do it."

"You are indeed fortunate," Xiang-hua said. "Have you ever met He Da's boss? Does your son ever talk about him?"

"No. He doesn't talk about his work. He's mentioned an

older man that seems to be important, but that's all," Er-nu said.

"An older man?" Xiang-hua couldn't remember Shu-chang mentioning an older man at the wine shop.

"Yes. A strange fellow. From what I gather, the man is blind. Blind! Now, isn't that odd?" she asked rhetorically. She raised her eyebrows as if in amazement and shook her head. Then, after that unexpected announcement, she turned to pick up her basket. Without waiting for a response, she said goodbye and proceeded down the lane to her fields.

Xiang-hua turned to Yao-sheng's house with a heavy heart, the neighbor's gossip about Ms. Chen ringing in her ears. It was neither what she expected nor wanted to learn. Before knocking on the door, she steeled her reserve. The neighbor had delivered a mixture of rumor and observation. There may be other reasons behind all that coming and going. She had to discover the truth.

Ms. Chen's delight at seeing her did not alleviate the dread building in Xiang-hua's chest. If anything, it only increased her morose mood.

Sitting on the brick kang with cups of hot water and the plate of steamed buns between them, the two young women chatted. About the art of making a good steamed bun. About the body being moved to a nearby temple. About Ms. Chen's relief that people no longer came around the house. Finally, Xiang-hua gathered her courage to ask about Ms. Chen's affair with the herbalist.

"Certainly not!" she exclaimed at the question. Her head snapped up. "How could you ask such a thing? Do you think because I'm poor, I've no honor?"

"I am only asking because there is a rumor going around.

It's important to clear this up so the court doesn't get involved." Xiang-hua soothed. "It's best if you tell me everything now, so I can help you. Was your husband involved in this, too?"

Ms. Chen's defiance wilted. She grasped her clay cup tightly in her hands. "My husband owed a lot of money and was in trouble. When Shi found out, he offered to lend enough to pay off the debt. At a price."

"Your favors?"

The young wife's head and shoulders barely moved in silent agreement.

"When did this start?"

"Four months ago."

"Are you still seeing Shi?"

"No. A few weeks ago, out of the blue, Yao-sheng told me to never let Shi into the house again. He was angry. Furious. I'd never seen him so mad. He said he needed more money, but Shi wouldn't lend him any. My favors weren't enough. My husband beat me because he said I was of no use." She wiped away a tear rolling down her cheek. "A few days after Shi turned him down for the loan, my husband became moody and distracted. And less angry. He never mentioned needing the loan again."

"What about that murdered fellow? Did your husband sell him your favors?"

Ms. Chen stared at Xiang-hua as if uncomprehending. Then, "No. But I did know him. Yao-sheng hired him to do repair work around the house. Although where he got the money for that, I don't know."

Delighted to find someone who admitted to knowing the victim, Xiang-hua asked, "Who was he? What's his name?"

"I was never introduced to him or even talked to him. I don't know any more than I told you. I don't know where he was from or his name."

Her response disappointed Xiang-hua, but the doctor persisted in her questioning. "Did you know if Shi might have had any enemies?"

"He never mentioned enemies. He was a kind man. He did a lot of good in his work. He helped so many people. Who could be his enemy?"

Xiang-hua was taken aback. Her husband sold her favors to the herbalist, yet she was defending Shi. The complexities of these relationships challenged her own upbringing in how people should and did behave. Nevertheless, trying to keep focused on the case, she asked, "No one? Are you sure?"

Ms. Chen's brow wrinkled in thought. "Well, there's a young farmer. It's very sad. He came for a cure for his wife who'd just given birth. Unfortunately, she died anyway. The baby survived. I understand he's blaming Shi for his wife's death." She turned away for a moment, then faced Xiang-hua again. "But, that's ridiculous! How can he blame Shi?" She sighed. In a softer voice she said, "I remember him. Such a loss. He's truly suffering, I'm sure. Still, I never heard him threaten Shi."

Xiang-hua watched as the young woman picked at the back of her rough hands and waited for her to continue.

When Ms. Chen finally spoke again, her voice was dispassionate. "It was his bad fate, that's all. Shi wasn't at fault. He couldn't be. He's a good man."

Xiang-hua tried not to show surprise at the depths of Ms. Chen's loyalty to Shi. How could this be, considering the circumstances of her being handed over to him? Or maybe it was *because* of the circumstances. Xiang-hua silently fumed at the abuse she suffered at the hands of both men. First, her heartless husband turned her, his own wife, into a prostitute. And then Shi participated in the money-making scheme. But here Ms. Chen sat, apparently claiming that because of Shi's kindness, she genuinely cared for him. It made Xiang-hua wonder if anyone else had ever shown her kindness.

"So, you never saw anyone arguing with the herbalist?"

"I didn't say that. Xin Fen-peng came around Shi's house twice. Drunk. He stood in front of the house, out on the road, yelling and accusing Shi of terrible things." Her hands danced around as if swatting bad words away.

"What kind of things?"

"He accused Shi of trying to mess with his wife, Lady Jiang. Very embarrassing." She bit her lip and shook her head.

"What did Shi do?"

"Do? What could he do? The man was drunk. Shi ignored him. Never even came to the door. Left Fen-peng on the street."

"What happened next?"

"Eventually, he left."

Embarrassing, yes. But what, if anything, did it have to do with the murder victim? Xiang-hua left feeling more frustrated than when she'd come.

CHAPTER 18

Leaving Huai-liang behind, Shu-chang and his friends again headed for the Shou Road neighborhood and the Flying Crane.

Stepping inside the wine shop, the quartet paused briefly, straining to see the clientele as their eyes adjusted to the muted light. Shu-chang coughed. Men filled the tables, crowding the room and making it difficult for the small, open windows to clear away the odors of sweat and stale wine.

Shu-chang looked over the scene, which was beginning to look familiar. The old, blind fellow perched at the table closest to the entrance, surrounded by a group of rough-looking men. The sounds of a smattering of able-bodied men gambling noisily in the far corner mixed with the chatter of clusters of men scattered around the room.

As he started forward, a gravelly voice called out from the side: "Ah, Teacher. You honor us once more with your presence."

Shu-chang turned. A burley man rose from among the men sitting at the first table. As he left the table and approached, he cast a smirk back at his friends.

"He Da. Good to see you," Shu-chang said.

"Still nosing around?" While his mouth smiled, his eyes stared hard at Shu-chang.

"We still haven't identified the victim, if that's what you mean. The only thing we know for sure is that he had gang symbols on him: a tattoo on his arm."

"Tattoos mean nothing. Anyone could get one as a protection against harm," He Da broke in.

"Would you get one?" Shu-chang challenged.

"Nah." He pushed his right sleeve up, revealing an unblemished arm. "See." He jerked his shoulder and his sleeve fell back into place. "I didn't say everyone would get a tattoo, only that it's not uncommon." A toothy grin and toss of the head accentuated his arrogance.

Shu-chang persisted. "And a white feather was found near him. It could have been dislodged from his hat by the pig when it attacked him," he said, pushing down a queasy sensation as an image of the mutilated body swam into view. He gulped back the bile rising in his throat while stubbornly staring at the white feather protruding from He Da's hat band.

"Pigeons are not uncommon in our little town," he said, ignoring Shu-chang's challenge.

"And then there is the protective Fu talisman. It looks like he was a member of a gang and needed lots of protection."

"Would you and your friends like to sit, Sir," the tavern owner asked Shu-chang as he came between the two men.

Shu-chang said "Yes" without taking his eyes off He Da.

He Da grinned. "I'll join you. Perhaps I have something that might be of interest."

Shu-chang's eyebrows shot up. He nodded and followed the owner, his men trailing close behind. He Da picked up his cup from the table and came to join them.

As they settled down, a yell went up from one of the gambling tables. A heavy-set man with a bright red face rose unsteadily to his feet. "You cheated!" He shouted as he lunged at a man sitting next to him. His fellow players quickly grabbed him and forced him back into his chair, their voices loud but unintelligible in the noisy room.

Shu-chang's attention reverted to He Da. "What do you have to tell me?" He expected He Da to tell him about the dead man's gang activities, because it was obvious the burley fellow was a leader in the White Feather Gang and, Shu-chang guessed, the victim was one of his followers. He rubbed his hands together in expectation. Finally, a break in the case.

"You know that fellow, Yao-sheng, who lives next door?"

Shu-chang nodded, perplexed.

"He has a wife. Have you seen her? Lovely. Not a real beauty, but comely." He bounced his head back and forth as if further assessing her. "Rumor has it that, even though times have been hard, Yao-sheng never seemed to be short of money, until recently ... You get my drift?"

Shu-chang stared at him. This conversation made no sense. What did this have to do with the murder? What did Yao-sheng's wife have to do with anything? Trying hard not to betray his confusion, Shu-chang said, "Times are hard for every farmer. Why is it worse for him?"

He Da laughed. "He's accumulated a serious gambling debt." He spat on the ground. The spittle landed perilously close to Shu-chang's feet. "He's been selling his wife's affections for extra money, but now his debt is more than she can bring in."

"Hmm," Shu-chang said. He tried to keep an unreadable countenance, but he was shocked. Would a simple farmer risk everything by prostituting his own wife?

He Da went on forcefully: "Yao-sheng is a gambler, and

gamblers never know when to quit." He Da rubbed his chin. "Selling his wife's favors is one thing, but, with his increasing debt, he's now going even further." He leaned toward Shu-chang and loudly whispered, "He's been asking around to see if anyone wanted a concubine. Bigger money, faster." He sat back and sneered. "It's amazing what some people will do, ain't it?"

Zhou, sitting on Shu-chang's left, leaned over. "I'd also heard such gossip from some of the men in the taverns."

Shu-chang looked over at him.

Zhou shrugged his shoulders. "I didn't think it was important. The body was found at the herbalist's, not Yao-sheng's."

"How do you know about his gambling debt? Who did he owe money to?" Shu-chang asked He Da.

"I don't know anything about who he owes money to. Could be anyone. But Yao-sheng's been frantically going all around trying to lay his hands on a bunch of money." He grinned. "The turtle was scared. Not paying a gambling debt is serious. No telling what might happen to a man that squirms out of his obligations." He Da pushed back in his chair and laughed.

Leaving the Flying Crane, Zhou walked next to Shu-chang; Lin and Fang stayed close behind. Each man's face expressed a look of concern and deep thought.

"Why do you think He Da told you all that about Yao-sheng? I don't get it," Zhou said.

"Perhaps he wanted to distract us from delving more deeply into the White Feather Gang. He Da has to be one of their leaders," Shu-chang said.

"He didn't have a tattoo on his arm," Lin pointed out.

"But he had a white feather in his cap, and the other men in the tavern all seem to give way to him," Fang said.

"Right. So, even though he doesn't have the tattoo, I'd say he was their leader," Shu-chang said.

"Still, why that whole yarn about Shi's neighbor? Who cares? It doesn't have anything to do with that man's death," Zhou insisted.

"Because the body was in herbalist Shi's pigpen and not Yao-sheng's?" Fang asked.

Zhou grunted an affirmative.

Shu-chang halted and the others clustered around him. "What if putting the body into herbalist Shi's pen was a mistake? What if it was supposed to be dumped into Yao-sheng's pen? They are close together. At night, in the dark, the killer could have simply made a mistake and thrown the body over the wrong wall."

"Ha!" The three others exhaled as one and their faces lit up at the suggestion.

"Nevertheless," Shu-chang continued, "there remains the question of who the victim was. Until we know that, we won't be able to figure out why he was killed and by whom."

A gloom settled back over Zhou, Lin, and Fang.

They ambled on in silence for a short time until Shu-chang asked, "Who was that blind fellow in there? He was at the same table the last time we visited the Flying Crane."

"He's certainly an odd one," Zhou said. "I always see him in there. The tavern must be his home away from home."

"Where does he live?" Shu-chang asked.

"No idea. I've seen him on the streets occasionally. Can't miss him because he carries that heavy staff to feel his way. But I don't know where he lives. He could sleep in an abandoned temple or rent a bed somewhere. Not uncommon for single men. Whatever's cheap or free."

"I saw him give a troublemaker the what-for when the fellow dared to accost him in the street," Lin volunteered.

"I remember that," Fang said.

"What happened?"

The two chuckled. "It wasn't pretty," Fang said. "You saw the stick he uses to help him walk, didn't you? He always has it with him. When that good-for-nothing started to make trouble, the old guy bashed him so hard across his chest that he crashed into the dirt." He shook his head, laughing. "That man may be old and blind, but he's fast. It was all over before you could blink. The bully had no idea what he'd gotten into. He fell like a downed log and that blind guy just kept on walking."

"I wonder if we should try to talk to him," Shu-chang said.

"We could, but I don't know how he'd help us. He can't see, and I've never heard him speak. He might be mute, too," Zhou said.

"Yeah," Lin said. "He never uttered a sound when he beat that guy with his stick. Just struck and calmly continued to wander down the street."

"Too bad. If he spends so much time at the Flying Crane, he must hear a lot. People wouldn't bother to hide anything from him," Shu-chang said. He raised his chin and looked around. "Before we leave the neighborhood, let's break up again into twos. Lin and Fang, you go together. Zhou, come with me. We need to get to the bottom of the murder. And quickly."

Shu-chang and Zhou tried talking with several men in the neighborhood, but to no avail. Everyone seemed to be suspicious and alert. Their eyes darted around the lane, watching to see if anyone was taking notice of them, worried that someone might see or hear them talking about the dead man. The exercise was futile. Out of energy, Shu-chang finally gave up.

As they moved through the streets, they saw a food cart with a vendor selling soup. Without needing to discuss it, they stopped for a snack. They stood near the cart, slurping their soup. Shu-chang tried once more to gather information and began quizzing the vendor.

"I can't help you identify the body found in Shi's pigsty," the peddler said. He turned away to ladle soup for another customer, who took the bowl and dropped down on his haunches to eat, eyeing Shu-chang and Zhou as he did so.

"You talking about that dead man?" the new fellow asked. "The one who used to work for Yao-sheng?"

Shu-chang nodded. "Do you know him?

"No, but I saw him standing near Shi's and Yao-sheng's places, arguing with that young farmer. What's his name?" He frowned down at his bowl, then looked up. "Huai-liang. That's it. Huai-liang. The one whose wife died."

"Do you know what they were arguing about?"

"Something about collecting money." He glanced around and stood up. He stepped closer to Shu-chang and dropped his voice. "I don't know that dead guy's name, but I've seen him around here, too. He collected debts that didn't get paid on time."

"What kind of debts?"

"Gambling debts, mostly, but also debts due merchants. The guy was tough. One day, I saw him grab Huai-liang's carrying pole and throw the food he was taking to market all over the road. When the farmer tried to fight back, the thug stomped on his baskets and threatened him. The tough guy said if he didn't come up with the money, anything could happen. Then he smashed the produce with his feet and asked if he understood."

Once they'd left the vendor and his food cart, Zhou shook his head. "That doesn't look good for Huai-liang."

Shu-chang nodded but didn't reply. He walked along lost in thought. Was that the connection he was looking for? Money and murder?

CHAPTER 19

Xiang-hua's conversation with Ms. Chen the day before left her with more questions, so she was once more making her way over to visit with Yao-sheng's wife. As she moved along the well-trodden path between the small family homesteads, a tall, wiry figure caught her attention. Heavy, covered baskets swung from the ends of the bamboo pole balanced on his right shoulder. His loose, heavy, cotton jacket flapped rhythmically against his sides.

"Huai-liang, how good to see you," Xiang-hua said in greeting.

Huai-liang grinned, revealing a missing front tooth. "Sister."

"How is your son doing?" she asked.

The grin died on his lips. "He's being kept by my brother. His wife had a baby not long ago, so she is able to feed my son too."

How fortunate, Xiang-hua thought. If not for his lactating sister-in-law, his son would have joined his wife in the after-life. "That is good," was all she could say.

He gently placed his burden on the ground and pushed his

sleeves up, revealing taut, sunburned arms. He rubbed his forehead. "Living with my brother's family has saved me."

Xiang-hua read deep sorrow in his eyes. The death of his wife had been so unexpected. He had done what he thought he should do in her time of sickness by seeking the help of herbalist Shi. But to no avail.

"Shi didn't treat her right. She'd just given birth and needed strength. He gave her the wrong medicine."

"What did she take?" Xiang-hua asked.

Huai-liang searched the sky as if looking for the answer. Finally, he listed several herbs that his wife used to make tea. Xiang-hua listened and considered each one. Shi's recommendations were typical of what would be given to a woman recovering from a difficult birth. They assisted in building qi. However, Xiang-hua knew that—even with the best of care— unforeseen complications could still arise suddenly and put the woman's life at risk. It didn't sound to her that the medicines could have been at fault.

Huai-liang slapped his fist into his hand, as if reliving his grief and anger. "Shi allowed my wife to die. He as much as killed her himself. Yet, he demands payment for his failed treatment. Payment that will bankrupt me and my family. Where's the justice in that?" he demanded. "And now, with that man turning up dead at Shi's, who knows what will happen? Anyone could be blamed for the death."

"Zhong and his team are still investigating. They'll discover who the real culprit is," Xiang-hua said. What could she say? There were no words to relieve him of his pain at losing his wife or his worry over a debt that could ruin his family. Whatever she said would be inadequate.

"I talked to Teacher Shu-chang and went to the temple for divine intervention," he went on. "I must protect my name, my son, my family."

As they talked, a figure moving toward them caught her

attention. His purposeful gate was familiar. Shu-chang. She pushed a lock of hair that had come loose back behind her ear and straightened her collar.

Huai-liang, noticing that she'd become distracted, also looked down the road. "Morning, Teacher," he called out.

Shu-chang greeted them as he approached. With a glance at Xiang-hua, he said: "You're out early."

"I have several clients to see today," she said. Even though this was a simple exchange, it made her uncomfortable. Was he criticizing her for being out on the road—alone—or giving her credit for starting work so early? And why did she care what he thought about that anyway?

"Did you write up my complaint for the court?" Huai-liang asked. His gaze slipped from Xiang-hua to Shu-chang, who shook his head.

"The official forms have not yet arrived. When they do, I will send for you. It may be a few days. We can't rush the yamen clerks. It's essential to keep to protocol."

Huai-liang frowned but nodded. "I want to get my complaint in before Zhong sends in his report on the murder. Otherwise, it will look like I'm responding to the security chief's report."

"How can his report involve you? Your problem is with Shi, not the victim," Xiang-hua said. "Perhaps you should let sleeping dogs lie."

The farmer glared at her. Returning to Shu-chang, he said, "Please let me know when the forms come. I can meet with you at any time. Any time."

"Of course," Shu-chang said.

Huai-liang bent down to retrieve his pole and his burden. When he stood up, he bowed to Shu-chang and gave Xiang-hua a curt nod before striding away.

His vehement, unprovoked behavior and comments caused Xiang-hua to wonder why he was so sure he'd be implicated in the murder. Was it because of a guilty conscience? She studied the muscular figure as he continued down the road, baskets smoothly undulating with each step.

"A strange man," Shu-chang said. "He isn't thinking straight. I only hope that by the time the official papers arrive, he's gained some perspective and gives up on this obsession with Shi. The debt they are arguing over is a private affair. Not a matter for the courts."

As the rigid form rounded a curve and disappeared from sight, Xiang-hua nodded in agreement. "Flailing out at the herbalist won't bring back his wife. He told me what Shi gave her. Common herbs. Nothing dangerous."

"She was awfully young to die so suddenly, though," Shu-chang said.

"Giving birth is a difficult time for a woman. It was her first child and she didn't have a mid-wife to see her through and help with the period after birth." She shook her head, but added, "Nevertheless, Shi should have checked on her to make sure she wasn't having a bad reaction to his herbs—which could happen even with common ones—or that the herbs were of no use. In either case, he should have changed his prescription."

"Well," Shu-chang changed the subject, "where are you going at this time of day?"

"To Ms. Chen's. I want to talk to her some more. I'm sure she's not been completely forthright with me so far." She held up her basket. "I've brought a snack to share. It may make her more comfortable with me. Besides, I feel she needs to confide in somebody. It might as well be me." She smiled up at Shu-chang and caught him staring at her. His eyes contained a warmth that struck her. She quickly dropped her own gaze to the road.

Shu-chang cleared his throat. "I'll have to finish up with classes today. When you've completed your rounds let's meet and discuss our findings. Zhong hasn't been able to find out anything, but between the two of us we seem to be picking up helpful information, piece by piece."

Afraid she might be blushing at the compliment, she lost her voice temporarily. A rare occurrence for her. Instead of responding, she nodded while busily rearranging the cloth over the top of her basket.

"See you later," he said and continued down the path.

She took a deep breath and approached Yao-sheng and Ms. Chen's house.

Ms. Chen beamed when she answered the knock on her door and saw Xiang-hua standing there. "Sister, come in." She opened the door fully to allow her to pass into the murky interior.

"I had to come down this way and decided to stop in and check on you." Xiang-hua held up the basket. "I also have a few extra tea cakes." She handed the basket over to Ms. Chen, who grasped it with two hands.

"You're too kind. Come in. Come in." She moved back into the dim room. "I'm doing fine. Your medicine made all the difference. I slept straight through the night, and I wasn't the least tired when I got up to make my husband's morning meal." She chatted on as she lit a fire in the stove to warm the water kettle.

Xiang-hua settled down on the kang, tucking her legs under her. From what she'd gleaned from the neighbors, the young wife kept to herself, not leaving the house unless she went to work in the fields, which she did almost daily. Her shoulders and arms exhibited the effects of such consistent, hard physical work. No gentlewoman would have the muscles she had. Yet, farm work did not bring her friendships. Xiang-hua had gleaned the young wife had no women friends in the neighborhood. Word was that her husband forbade her talking to the other women. He believed women's talk was mere gossip and could only cause trouble.

After chatting while drinking the hot water and nibbling on the tea cakes, Xiang-hua broached the reason for her visit. "From what you've told me, herbalist Shi has been very kind to you."

Ms. Chen's eyes focused on a middle distance. She nodded.

"He must have been unhappy when Yao-sheng stopped allowing him to visit you."

"Uhm-hm. My husband did that because Shi wouldn't lend him any more money. Yao-sheng became afraid. The people he owed wanted him to pay up. He said they'd cripple him, if not kill him, if he didn't pay."

"So why didn't Shi lend him more money? Why stop now? Then things could have gone on as usual."

Pursing her mouth, Ms. Chen refocused on Xiang-hua's face and was silent for a long time. Xiang-hua waited. Finally, exhaling a long sigh, Ms. Chen said: "Shi didn't want my husband to be able to pay his debt. He told me that if those thugs killed Yao-sheng, I would be free. We could be together."

A new wrinkle. Xiang-hua touched her forehead and took a moment to grasp everything Ms. Chen told her. What a convoluted mess this case was. What did all these entanglements mean? Strangely, as with much of the information they'd gathered so far, this made Shi the most likely victim of murder, not the stranger found in his pigsty. Xiang-hua took a deep breath and continued her questioning.

She'd only had a short conversation with Shu-chang last night. His discoveries at the tavern confirmed their earlier information about Yao-sheng's intentions to use his wife as a way of canceling his debts.

"Gossip has it that your husband called you his only asset. That he intended to sell you as a concubine to a traveling merchant. Did you know that?"

A tear slipped down Ms. Chen's cheek. She angrily slapped at it, pushing it away.

Xiang-hua persisted. "Did Shi know that? If Yao-sheng sold you, he'd have money to cover his debt. Shi would never see you again." Even as she pushed ahead, Xiang-hua's conscience tugged at her. Was it right for her to purposefully upset Ms. Chen? A young wife no older than herself. Abused. Alone. With no family and no friends. To cause pain—any kind of pain—was not what her grandmother had taught her. It was the antithesis of being a doctor.

Ms. Chen fiercely pouted, her eyes scrunched into mere slits. "Shi came over one night after my husband went to the Flying Crane. He told me the gossip about my husband's plan. I didn't know anything before that. How could he do such a thing? I'm his wife," she said, clasping her hands tightly together, ignoring the tears now freely streaming down her cheeks.

Xiang-hua cringed at the irony of Ms. Chen's comment.

"When Shi told me, I burst out crying. He thought I knew. But I didn't. I didn't."

"What did Shi expect you to do?"

Ms. Chen glared through red-rimmed eyes. "What could I do? It's against the law to sell your wife. Yet, how could I go to court with a complaint against my husband? It's unheard of. It's not lawful." Her voice rose. "There's nothing I could do.

"Shi told me he would take care of it." With the flat of her hand, she scrubbed her face clean of tears and looked defiantly at Xiang-hua.

"'Take care of it.' What did he mean?"

"That he would take care of my husband. I thought he meant he would poison him," she said. "He grew many herbs that could be used as poisons if too strong a dose was eaten or drunk."

CHAPTER 20

P*ound. Crush. Scrape.*
  Pound. Crush. Scrape.

Xiang-hua fiercely pulverized the seeds, driven on by the pestle's thump against the mortar. She'd been pounding, crushing, and scraping for some time. Her hand and arm protested. She continued on. Earthenware containers filled with fine powders.

"What a racket you're making!"

Pestle in midair, Xiang-hua stopped and turned. Xiao-ren stood in the doorway, hands on hips.

"What are you doing here?"

"I was trying to study, but all this noise drove me to distraction. I had to stop."

"Ha. You were looking for an excuse not to do your lessons, that's all. Anything not to study." She tried to look stern but a smile tugged at the corners of her mouth. Her brother was energetic. Too energetic to find studying quietly at his desk at all satisfying. It was only his admiration and commitment to Teacher Shu-chang that caused him to even try to learn his lessons.

Xiao-ren sauntered over and stared down at the table covered with small mounds of seeds, dried leaves, and bowls and jugs of various sizes. "You'll never get all of that," he waved a hand over the seeds and leaves, "ground up if you keep up this way. Your hand will give out."

"So, you're the doctor now?"

He looked at her. "You know I'm right. What's wrong? Are you angry?" His voice mirrored the surprise in his face.

Xiang-hua vigorously shook her head. Everyone always expected her to be the quiet one. Restrained. Always respectful. She prided herself on maintaining proper deportment at all times. But Xiao-ren was right. When she came into the lab to prepare medicines for her visit to Lady Jiang's, Xiang-hua had begun the morning's tasks with a clear mind. However, as she remembered their last meeting, Xiang-hua thought about how Lady Jiang refused medical assistance. That thought poked at the young doctor until she had to admit she was angry. Angry at herself. Angry at Lady Jiang. Didn't she trust her skills? Sure, she wasn't her grandmother, but she'd studied. Learned at the feet of her grandmother, the best women's doctor in the country.

Even the Emperor valued her grandmother's ability. He brought her to the palace to care for the women in his household. Xiang-hua was her protégé. If people didn't have confidence in her, in her skills, her grandmother would lose face. How could she fail?

Xiang-hua laid the pestle on the long, worn, wooden table. Her shoulders dropped. She stared at the seeds and poked a finger into them. "Lady Jiang isn't well, yet she won't let me heal her."

Xiao-ren cocked his head. "That's it? That's what's wrong?"

"Don't you understand? I was called over to help her

mother-in-law. When I realized that Lady Jiang herself needed medical treatment and tried to help, she refused."

Xiao-ren grimaced. "Listen to yourself. You just said you were called over there to help her mother-in-law. Everyone knows that taking care of the old woman is everything to her. She wouldn't have asked for you if she didn't trust you."

Xiang-hua looked at him. "Perhaps you're right."

"Of course I'm right!" he said, opening his eyes wide as if to say, *How could you doubt me?*

But Xiang-hua still couldn't let go of her doubts, remembering that it was Fen-peng, not Lady Jiang, who'd requested that she come to tend his mother. "But why wouldn't Lady Jiang let me treat her when she is so obviously in pain?"

"Maybe she's worried about money. Before her husband returned from his extended business trip, Lady Jiang was selling her own jewelry to buy coal and food for her mother-in-law."

Xiang-hua frowned. "You shouldn't spread such gossip."

"Well, it's true. Everyone knows anyhow. It's not like it's a secret."

"But Fen-peng is back now. Money shouldn't be a problem."

Xiao-ren paused for a moment before saying, "Well, as we know, rumor has it that Fen-peng didn't do well in his business and he came home broke. Even so, he spends more time partying and drinking than working."

"I've seen him once at the house. He appeared to be a fine, well-spoken gentleman," Xiang-hua said.

Xiao-ren snickered. "You should see him drunk. He easily slips into angry bullying."

"His mother did indicate he drank excessively, but neither woman suggested he was violent."

Xiao-ren shrugged. "It still means he's recklessly wasting the family's money."

Xiang-hua suddenly cupped her forehead in her palm. "Of course, I understand," she said. "Lady Jiang couldn't say anything to me about family finances without causing her husband to lose face. She would sacrifice anything for Old Madam but not for her own needs. Now I know what to do to help Lady Jiang without causing her to feel disrespectful toward her husband." She looked at her brother and slapped her hands sharply together. "Thank you so much. Who knew such a young scoundrel could be so smart?" Laughing, she reached out and messed his hair.

"Don't be so polite," Xiao-ren said with uncharacteristic modesty, ducking her enthusiastic friskiness. His face glowed at her praise.

Xiang-hua immediately started scurrying around the lab to gather herbs, which she then carefully mixed together and poured into a couple of small vessels.

"What are you doing?" Xiao-ren asked.

"I'm going over to see Lady Jiang. She needs me. I can help. We can always work out the money part." She began to fill her medicine bag.

"You're taking a lot of things. Are they all for Lady Jiang?"

Xiang-hua smiled. "She is suffering from more than her leg infection. She also suffers from excessive dampness; therefore, her spleen is out of balance. I will need to treat both to make her well again." With that, she tossed on a short jacket, shouldered her bag, grabbed her wide-brimmed hat, and strode out the door.

This time it was Lady Jiang's mother-in-law who greeted Xiang-hua as she entered the women's quarters. Her pale face had begun to take on a healthier color. "As you can see, I'm much improved, thanks to your excellent care." She put aside an embroidery project she had been working on. Her eyes were bright and clear.

"You are too kind," Xiang-hua said, pleased to see the older woman sitting up in a carved wooden chair.

She read the Old Madam's pulse. "You are getting stronger. That's good. I will give you another moxibustion treatment today. We do not want your qi to revert to its weakened state. Once you are in balance, you may rely on the medicine and my prescribed diet to keep in good health."

After the treatment, the two women sat drinking tea. Xiang-hua looked to the adjoining door. "I was hoping to see Lady Jiang today, too. Is she out?"

The elderly woman pursed her lips and wrung her hands. "She is not well, I'm afraid. She has a fever and—although she denies it—appears to be in pain. I'm afraid she's not healing from when she cut her leg to make my medicinal soup." The old woman's eyes teared up. "She is the most filial of daughters-in-law."

As she said this, a noise coming down the veranda caught her attention. *Shirr, thump. Shirr, thump.* Lady Jiang soon appeared in the doorway.

"How kind of you to visit us again. I didn't expect to see you so soon," Lady Jiang said, favoring her right leg as she limped into the room and joined the two.

"We've just finished a moxibustion treatment," Old Madam said. "I'm feeling so much better."

"Yes," Lady Jiang said to Xiang-hua, "We owe you much for bringing her back to her normal self." She smiled fondly at her mother-in-law.

"And now I want to have a look at your leg, Lady Jiang," Xiang-hua said standing and coming to the other woman's side. Not giving Lady Jiang a chance to demur, Xiang-hua went on: "If I don't do my duty as a doctor, I will be failing my grandmother and the responsibilities she's placed in me." Knowing how important filial piety was to Lady Jiang, Xiang-hua used it as tool in her argument to care for her. To interfere with Xiang-hua's obligations toward her own grandmother just to avoid the expense of a medical treatment would be difficult for Lady Jiang.

"I thought it had begun to heal," Lady Jiang weakly asserted as Xiang-hua began her examination of the wound.

To get a piece of her flesh, she had made a deep cut on her upper thigh. She hadn't spared herself. Her body was hot to the touch. The area was a livid red and a cloudy fluid continued to drain from the wound. Xiang-hua prepared a poultice, generously applied it over and around the wound, and wrapped a cloth around the leg to hold it in place. She silently read Lady Jiang's pulse. "In addition to the infection, you are suffering from excess dampness." The results were as she expected. Reaching over to her medicine bag, she took out a small earthen jar with a stopper. "Drink this in a cup of hot water three times a day."

Noting that Lady Jiang still appeared resistant, Xiang-hua said, "You cannot care for your honorable mother-in-law if you are sick yourself. It is your responsibility. Who will care for her if you don't guard your own health?"

For a moment, Lady Jiang let her gaze rest on her hands, which she clasped tightly together in her lap. "I thought this was my punishment." Her voice was barely a whisper.

"Punishment? For what?" her mother-in-law asked. Old Madam's wrinkled brow reflected her perplexity.

Xiang-hua leaned forward to catch every faintly spoken word.

Lady Jiang looked up. "For jealousy. I'm sorry," she said to her mother-in-law. "I've tried and tried. I've always been jealous of the time and attention my husband pays to those women in the flower houses." She gulped. "I understand when he's away for months at a time. But even now, when he's home?"

"My daughter," Old Madam said softly.

"In the Book of Filial Piety, it says that one of the worst things a wife could do is be jealous." She lightly passed her fingers over the cloth covering her wound. "Even with *gegu*, my stubborn, jealous nature created disharmony and caused problems. But now," her chin lifted, "things will be different. I understand what I must do to overcome my grievous short-comings.

"Last night the deity Lord Guan, the embodiment of righteousness, came to me." Her eyes shone as she relived her experience. "He explained why I am constantly unwell and why, although done for filial reasons, this," she passed her hand gently over the top of her leg, "would have trouble healing. I am atoning in this life for my evil deeds in a former life. In the past, as a young man, I had many advantages: I was from a wealthy family; I was educated and successful. But then, I murdered a young scholar. For that, I had to atone. Therefore, I was reborn as a woman, married an unsuccessful scholar, and suffer with a carousing husband." She released a long, steady breath.

"Lord Guan warned that jealousy leads to the destruction of the family. He ordered me to pray and to cleanse my heart. I kowtowed and promised I would. Then, he reached out and removed my tainted, jealousy-ridden heart and replaced it with a pure one." With a beatific smile, she tapped her chest with an open hand. "Now my heart is a precious, pure lotus pod. And I can now accept your care."

Xiang-hua stared at her patient. This outpouring was not what she had expected, but she understood that it meant from now on Lady Jiang would be willing to accept her medical advice and attention. And that was enough for Xiang-hua.

As the young doctor walked back to her lab, she thought about Lady Jiang, Old Madam, and Fen-peng. She thought about the thin membrane that divided the natural from the supernatural world. What would have happened to Lady Jiang if Xiang-hua hadn't returned today to care for her wound? What if it had been left untreated? She couldn't believe that it would have magically cured itself or that a spirit would cure it. But, then, what about her changing her mind and marching over to the house prepared to do whatever it took to get Lady Jiang the medical care she needed? Did her own actions come from an outside force she couldn't fathom?

CHAPTER 21

Shu-chang strode along the veranda leading to his classroom. Glancing over at the door to the women's quarters, he wondered if Xiang-hua had returned. Or maybe she was in her lab. He looked down the gallery toward a double door with elaborate latticework on its upper half. The lab had originally been used by both her grandfather and grandmother and was, therefore, separate from the women's quarters.

He wanted to check in with Xiang-hua, share the gossip he'd heard, and find out what she'd learned on her visits to Ms. Chen's and Lady Jiang's. If he was lucky, she'd be in the lab working. After living in the Xin compound for a few months, he had learned Xiang-hua's habit of spending nearly all her time in the lab.

He turned away from the women's quarters, walked past the classroom, and headed for the room at the end. As he approached the lab, he was disheartened by the silence. She must still be out. He'd have to wait.

A quiet rustling broke the stillness. Paper slipping over paper? He halted at the entrance and listened. Another, almost imperceptible, sound encouraged him. He knocked lightly on the door with its rice-paper-and-lattice windows.

Xiang-hua opened the door. She wore a dark green work jacket with a green embroidered scroll flowing around its collar and down its opening. Her hair was tied at the nape of her neck and hung loosely down her back. He inhaled the musty, vaguely herbal fragrance swirling around her. Her casual attire made her seem more approachable. As if he didn't have to keep the distance required between a young woman from a middle-class family and any male.

"I was hoping you'd be in, and we could talk—"

"—about the murder," Xiang-hua said, completing his sentence. She smiled up at him before returning to her workbench.

Leaving the doors wide open, he followed her into the airy room. Windows lining one side let in a bare suggestion of a breeze along with plenty of sunlight. The main worktable had been placed so as to receive maximum light from the open windows.

They sat on wooden stools near the table. A text with images and lists of herbs lay open. Sheets of paper were spread out on the table's surface. Fresh ink filled the ink stone. Xiang-hua had been studying.

"I haven't made much progress in identifying the victim, other than what we already know: that he was a gang member and followed Taoist practices," Shu-chang said. "I think He Da, the fellow I believe to be the White Feather Gang's leader, knows him, but he isn't talking."

Xiang-hua pursed her lips. "A neighbor said she'd seen the victim in the area for several days beforehand. He was working in and around Yao-sheng's. When the sun was hot, he'd take off his shirt. It was then that she saw tattoos on his arm. That alarmed her and convinced her that he was a potentially dangerous thug. She kept her young, unmarried daughter hidden back in the house when he was around."

"Did anyone else see him in the area?"

"Ms. Chen confirmed that he did some work for her husband. Although she claimed he never entered the house."

"And you believe her?"

Xiang-hua paused a moment before answering. "I don't know. She's holding something back, but I can't say what it is."

"Was she able to tell you more about the victim? His name? Where he came from?"

"No. She insisted she didn't know anything about him. He stayed outside and she never interacted with him.

"I've discovered a lot of motives for wanting people like the herbalist, or even Yao-sheng, dead, but not our unknown dead man!" Glancing over to the open windows, she took a deep breadth. "According to both the neighbor and Ms. Chen herself, Yao-sheng sold her favors to herbalist Shi." A deep red crept up her neck. She looked down at the scarred table-top, obviously embarrassed to have to discuss such a thing with her cousin.

Shu-chang shared her discomfort. But it couldn't be helped. It was a part of the case. Even though they didn't yet know what part. "I'd heard the same in the wine shop. And more." He paused and rubbed his hand over his mouth. "Rumor has it that Yao-sheng was planning to sell his wife as a concubine."

Xiang-hua wrinkled her nose in distaste. "Ms. Chen knew that. Shi knew it, too. He came to her and told her that he'd *take care of* her husband. Implying—at least she believed—that he'd poison Yao-sheng, and she'd be free to be with him. Further, from what I understood in talking to her, she knew about it for several days, if not longer." She tapped her fingers on the rim of a clay bowl sitting on the work table.

"If Shi tried to poison Yao-sheng, how would he get him to eat or drink it?" Shu-chang asked.

"Right. That's the big question. Yao-sheng wouldn't trust the herbalist at this point. Not when they are in the middle of this conflict."

"So it would have to be—" Shu-chang started.

"—given to him by his wife," Xiang-hua finished.

Shu-chang nodded. "Making her, along with her lover, directly responsible for her husband's death."

"Hmm. Interesting, but it still—" Shu-chang said.

"—doesn't explain why that stranger was killed." Xiang-hua said, looking up. "Yao-sheng is still alive and well."

Shu-chang nodded again. He watched Xiang-hua's face. Her expression reflected his own frustration with this case.

"And then there's Fen-peng," Xiang-hua went on. "Lady Jiang said he was extremely jealous of Shi because the herbalist visited her at home. And Ms. Chen told me that she had seen Fen-peng over at Shi's, threatening him. Drunk and angry. Not a good combination. Of course, Ms. Chen vehemently denies that there was anything between the herbalist and Lady Jiang. But then how would she know?" She pinched the bridge of her nose.

"Still, whether Fen-peng's suspicions had merit isn't important. Because, once more, none of this tells us anything about the victim and why *he* was killed," Shu-chang exhaled in exasperation. "We seem to have managed to uncover a couple of good motivations for killing the herbalist. If he turns up dead, we'll know where to look for his killer."

"And you were not able to get anyone at the Flying Crane or elsewhere on Shou Road to tell you more about the victim? No friends? No neighbors? Nothing?" She stared quizzically up at him.

Shu-chang realized she wasn't criticizing him. Nevertheless, it felt like a challenge. He clutched his hand into a fist.

"He Da caused everyone in the wine shop to shut down. Unless we can find one of those patrons on their own, away from unwanted ears, no one will dare speak up."

"Do you think He Da could have killed the victim?"

Shu-chang paused a moment, then shook his head. "I might be wrong, but I don't think so. He seemed angry about the man's death and how his body was treated. Thrown into a pigsty and mutilated."

Disappointment danced across Xiang-hua's face.

Shu-chang shifted around on the stool and tapped his index finger on the table. "There is one guy who I think could know a lot, but we can't talk to him."

"Because of He Da?"

He frowned. "Worse. The man's blind and probably mute."

It was Xiang-hua's turn to frown. "I've heard about that fellow. According to He Da's mother, he's accepted among the gang members and may even be a leader; they all show him deference. I don't know, though. How could he be a boss if he can't speak?" She let her fingers rest on the bowl's rim as she gave the latter some thought. Then she said, "Er-nu was probably mistaken. After all, she doesn't know him personally." She tapped the rim sharply in annoyance. "Still, how can a blind-mute tell us anything?"

"Well, he's a constant at the Flying Crane. He's got to hear everything. Who would worry about such a man being a threat? Even if he knew the most incriminating information." As he said this, Shu-chang realized how ridiculous it sounded. He was a blank wall. Things happened in front of it, but nothing left an imprint. Communication stopped there. He exhaled loudly and shook his head.

Xiang-hua pushed aside the papers on the table. "No one can exist in a vacuum. Even an outsider. Even a thug. Someone has to know him. I don't think I can find out anything more from Lady Jiang, Ms. Chen, or the neighbor woman. I think I have to go into the warren and talk to the women there."

Shu-chang's eyes widened, and he scowled at her.

Xiang-hua lifted her chin and met his gaze. "Women are often the eyes and ears of the neighborhood."

Shu-chang blew out a puff of air. *No wonder Uncle Xin worries about her. Why did she have to be so bold?* Talking to her patients was one thing; going into an unsafe neighborhood was unacceptable. While he valued working with her and respected her perspective, this was different. He would never put her in danger.

"I'm not questioning the value of their information. That's not the issue." He loudly tapped the table between them. "You can't possibly go into that den of thieves. You're a woman. It's dangerous. It's unseemly."

She glared back. "Before grandmother left for the capital, we visited several sick women in that area. She never refused to help where help was needed."

Shu-chang relented. A bit. He had no option. "I'm not criticizing your grandmother. She's an honorable elder. Her reputation goes before her. But you're young. Unmarried. Vulnerable. It's not the same for you. Don't you see that?"

To his dismay, Xiang-hua's lower lip shot out in defiance. She appeared to refuse his good counsel and, instead, chafed at his concern.

"And just how do you think you're going to get the women to open up to you? Have one of your trio pound on their doors and intimidate them into talking?"

"Now, don't be dramatic. Zhou, Lin, and Fang are good men."

"I'm sure. But they'll very likely be perceived as menacing nonetheless," she huffed.

Shu-chang sighed. He drummed his fingers on the table.

He had to admit that any of them going up to a family's door would not be a welcome sight to a woman. But, really, he couldn't just let her wander around by herself. Who knows what she'd run into? She might be smarter than any woman he'd ever met, but she was too innocent. Couldn't she understand how evil some people could be? Her naiveté would get her in serious trouble. He scrutinized her stubborn face as he thought of a solution.

"What if I go with you? You could ask the questions. I'd just be there," he finally said.

"No. They still won't speak up." She tapped her fingers on the table across from his hand.

"Xiao-ren can come with me," she said. Before Shu-chang could protest, she continued. "Unfortunately, he already knows, and is known throughout, the warren. He's my younger brother. No one will think it odd for us to be together when I visit grandmother's old clients." She shifted toward him. "Does that satisfy you?" she asked, looking up with mischievous, dark eyes.

It was obvious that she intended to go no matter what he said. He had to admit that this was the best he was going to get from her. And really, by using her contacts, they might finally be able to get a break in the investigation.

He gave in. "When can you go?"

CHAPTER 22

"Hey, Xiao-ren, ready for a game of dice?" a gaunt man cheerfully called out. His toothless smile faded, however, as he caught sight of Xiang-hua at the boy's side. Her serious countenance left no question about what she thought of his invitation.

Xiang-hua forbore scowling at either the gambler or her brother. At fifteen, he'd already become too well-known among the rough-and-tumble elements of the town. And the warren was their center. She hated his involvement and normally discouraged his ever coming here. She feared the influence such friends had on her brother's character. Still, today it was precisely this connection that made having Xiao-ren with her important in completing her mission of identifying the murder victim.

Through her apprenticeship training with her grandmother, Xiang-hua had visited a few families in the warren over the past few years. This was the first time she'd come without her grandmother, however. How would she be greeted? Few people paid attention to an apprentice. They were as any servant would be: ignored. Too unimportant to be noticed. Would people remember her and be willing to open up to her about such a sensitive topic?

Within a block of entering the neighborhood, she approached a time-worn building and knocked on its roughly hewn door. It soon opened, revealing a disheveled, middle-aged woman in a food-stained overblouse. She squinted at the duo silhouetted against the late afternoon sunlight. Her eyes quickly adjusted, and she greeted Xiang-hua warmly.

"Sister, how good to see you. But no one is sick here. We are all well, thanks to your grandmother."

"Madam Yi, I'm here on another matter," Xiang-hua said, relieved that the woman did remember her. "You've probably heard about the body found in herbalist Shi's pigpen."

The woman's face tightened.

"I'm asking around to see if anyone might know who the man was."

The woman glanced at Xiao-ren standing behind his sister and remained silent.

"He died anonymously and tragically. His soul will be unhappy," Xiang-hua said.

The woman looked pointedly at Xiao-ren. "You get around these parts. You don't know who he is?"

Xiao-ren shook his head.

She glanced back at Xiang-hua. "I've heard he could be an outsider who's been here a while. Some say he rented a bed at the widow Yang's house. Her husband died in the conflict with the Yuan Dynasty. She earns rice money renting out beds."

"Do you know her? Could you take us there?"

The woman turned and yelled, "I'm going out! I'll be back soon," into the room behind her. Stepping through the doorway and into the street, she said, "Follow me. It's not far."

Xiang-hua exchanged a look with Xiao-ren and they fell

in line with her. Xiang-hua's heart beat faster as she considered how easily and quickly they found someone who could identify the victim. Once they knew who the murdered man was, they would find his killer. Justice would be served, harmony restored, and his ghost could be at rest.

The three walked in a circuitous route through the dusty streets. Xiang-hua lost her sense of direction, but Xiao-ren moved confidently beside the woman and seemed to be familiar with the area. Eventually, they came to another beaten-down building with a sturdy, if crudely fashioned, door. The woman answering their knock was a duplicate of their guide: a middle-aged woman wearing a rumpled, stained over blouse. She looked old and worn for her years.

"Widow Yang. We've come to talk to you about your boarder," their guide said.

Widow Yang nodded as if she'd been expecting them. She stepped into the street to join them, closing the door behind her. The late afternoon rays highlighted the creases around her eyes and on her forehead. "He was a good man."

"What was his name?" Xiang-hua asked.

"Luo. Luo Yuan-jue. He's from the north. No family around here."

"Do you know where he worked?"

Pursing her lips in thought, she first shook her head. "He did odd jobs. Whatever he could get. He never had much money. He could usually be found at the Flying Crane. He did say He Da often hired him."

"Hired him?" Xiang-hua repeated.

Widow Yang glared at her. "You already know he was a gang member, right? What more do you need to know? You can make your own conclusions."

"Don't be offended. She's only looking to help give his spirit rest," Madam Yi interjected.

"Did he have any friends that you know of?" Xiang-hua said.

Widow Yang shuffled back and forth from foot to foot. She peered at Xiang-hua, quickly looked over at Madam Yi, and scanned the street behind them. "There was one fellow he often hung around with. Another northerner. Bai Hong. He rents a bed from Granny Yueh in that house." She pointed to a building across the street. "He's probably not there now, though. He and Yuan-jue usually left together and went to the Flying Crane. I suppose that's where he is now."

Xiang-hua looked at the house. "I would like to talk to Granny Yueh."

"I can introduce you to her, Sister," Widow Yang volunteered.

"Good. Let's go over," Xiang-hua said.

Xiang-hua and her growing coterie trooped across the street, Widow Yang in the lead.

As they approached the house, a figure moved away from its open window. The door immediately swung in at Widow Yang's knock.

"Granny Yueh," Widow Yang greeted the wizened figure outlined by the open doorway. "Sister Xiang-hua would like to talk to you about your boarder, Bai Hong."

The tiny, withered woman with bleary eyes stared up into Xiang-hua's face. "Ah, I know you. You study medicine under your honorable grandmother."

"I am her poor student," Xiang-hua said modestly.

"What do you need to know?" Granny Yueh asked. "If Hong is in trouble, I don't know anything about it. He sleeps here, that's all."

"He's not in trouble. We're trying to learn more about the dead man found at herbalist Shi's. I understand he and Hong were friends. I am hoping Hong may be able to help us."

Granny Yueh licked her chapped lips. "He's not here.

You'll find him at the Flying Crane. That's where they always go."

"So you knew Yuan-jue as well," Xiang-hua said.

Granny Yueh snorted. "Birds of a feather, those two," she said and cackled.

"Do you have any idea why someone would want to kill Yuan-jue?"

"No, I don't. I can tell you, though, that Hong probably won't be able to help you on that either. He's furious at his friend's death. If he had any idea who killed him, I'm sure that person wouldn't last the day." Her watery eyes looked up at Xiang-hua meaningfully.

"So you don't think Hong suspects anyone?"

"Yesterday, he and a couple of others were sitting around, talking, trying to figure out what happened. The last they'd heard, Yuan-jue picked up extra money doing a cushy job for that herbalist's neighbor. That's all."

Leaving Granny Yueh's, Xiang-hua thanked the women for helping them.

"Sure you don't need us anymore?" Widow Yang asked. "We're glad to come along." The other woman agreed with enthusiasm.

"Thank you, no. You've both been very helpful, though," Xiang-hua said, dismissing them. This was probably the most exciting thing they've done in a while. Their daily lives consisted of the same grinding boredom and struggle for a pittance. Nevertheless, she didn't want them to put them in unnecessary danger.

Heads together and chatting with broad hand gestures, the two women strolled away lost in their animated conversation.

"Xiao-ren, let's go to the Flying Crane," she said when the women were out of earshot.

"You can't go there. Women never go inside."

Xiang-hua seemed to study the middle distance momentarily. Maybe Shu-chang had had a point. Visiting women's homes was one thing; turning up in a wine shop was completely different.

Finally, she grinned. "I know. I'll stop in a nearby noodle shop while you go into the Flying Crane and ask questions."

Xiao-ren's face blanched. "I don't think so," he said. "It's not that I wouldn't like to help out by asking questions. But … going to the Flying Crane is like stepping into a tiger's mouth. They'll eat me alive."

The strength and sincerity of his reaction made her reconsider. She couldn't risk her little brother's safety. And anyway, they'd already gathered a lot of useful information about the dead man. "Let's go home and talk to Shu-chang," she said. "He and his friends can investigate further."

The two strolled back through the narrow streets, Xiao-ren leading the way. At an intersection, small carts and peddlers carried the last of the day's snacks in baskets swinging from bamboo poles balanced on their shoulder. A voice called to Xiang-hua.

"Sister, how good to see you!"

Xiang-hua swiveled toward a building with an old sign hanging over the door. They stood before the Joyful Garden, a down-at-the-heels brothel. Several adolescent girls sat along the building's outside wall. A plump woman stood up and waved.

Xiang-hua smiled. It was one of her grandmother's former patients.

"Jade, how have you been?" Xiang-hua returned as she walked toward the line of prostitutes.

"I'm well. With your honorable grandmother at the capital, you're working on your own now, eh?" She looked Xiang-hua over. "Could you examine my friend, Pearl?" She gestured toward a pale woman with dark circles ringing lusterless eyes.

"I don't have my medicine bag with me, but let me have a look."

Jade and the other women shuffled down the bench, leaving room for Xiang-hua to sit next to Pearl.

Xiao-ren stood uncomfortably next to his sister. "I don't think you should be seen here with them," he whispered, nodding his head toward the women on the bench.

"Nonsense. Grandmother treated them. I'll treat them."

"You're not Grandmother," he said.

Xiang-hua bristled. She knew what he meant: their grandmother was an elder; she was famous as a women's doctor. Xiang-hua was barely out of the first blush of youth. Being at a bordello, even as a doctor, could easily be misconstrued.

"It's my duty to carry on her work," Xiang-hua said and went to sit between Pearl and Jade on the bench.

Xiao-ren's face turned red as he watched his sister sitting amongst the Joyful Garden's working girls.

Ignoring her brother, Xiang-hua examined Pearl's face, reached for her wrist, and read her pulse. She asked a few questions and listened closely to the answers given by both Pearl and a couple of her friends nearby. Realizing that much of her condition was due to overwork and malnourishment, Xiang-hua recommended foods to eat and as much rest as possible. They all listened attentively, staring at her mouth as if memorizing every word that came out of it. They knew following the prescription would be difficult. The Joyful Garden's owner never changed the girls' schedules. None of them had money for fruit and the desired vegetables, much less meat and eggs. Nevertheless, they murmured assurances that she would be taken care of. They would try their best.

Xiang-hua started to leave. Jade leaned close to her. "Word is that you were the coroner for that dead guy found next to Yao-sheng's place." Her eyes rounded as she whispered these words. That a young, unmarried woman would take on such a job fascinated her.

Xiang-hua settled back down onto the bench, intrigued by how Jade had described the victim's location. Not in the herbalist's pigpen. Next to Yao-sheng's. She silently waited, examining the nodding heads of the women around her.

"Yao-sheng is well known here," Jade said.

"Jade's his favorite," one of the women volunteered. The others twittered assent. A shadow passed over Jade's eyes.

"He is obsessed with herbalist Shi," Jade said.

"Why? What has Shi done to offend him?" Xiang-hua asked.

"Yao-sheng is in debt because of his gambling habit. Everyone knows that. He blames Shi for it."

"How can that be? Shi doesn't gamble. Not that I've heard of, anyway," Xiang-hua said and cast a quick, questioning glance toward Xiao-ren.

Her brother shook his head. "I've never seen him gambling."

"He was Yao-sheng's bank. Yao-sheng used to brag about how much he got out of that man. Clothing. Food. Money. Lots of money. Silver and copper."

"So what happened?"

Jade shook her head. "I don't know why Shi stopped giving him gifts and lending him money. Yao-sheng never said. But a couple of weeks ago, he was very agitated. Said the guy he owed his gambling debt to demanded payment. Yao-sheng was nervous. Afraid. He cursed Shi." Jade shifted on the bench and faced Xiang-hua more directly. "About a week ago, he came in all calm and relaxed. He told me he'd worked out a plan to not only get money to pay off his debt, but to take over Shi's property as well." She stopped.

"Well, what was it?" Xiao-ren demanded impatiently.

"He wouldn't exactly say. What he did say was that it

involved hiring Yuan-jue. But, not for, you know, doing anything illegal, just to work on his house." She looked confused by her own description.

Xiang-hua studied the young woman and glanced over at the others on the bench. They all shared Jade's look of puzzlement.

"We already know that," Xiao-ren said. "That's not suspicious."

"Did he say why Yuan-jue? Or did he just want to hire anyone to work at his house?" Xiang-hua asked.

Jade bit her lip, thinking. "At first he said he wanted a laborer. Someone from outside our city. Someone unknown. Later, he hired Yuan-jue and seemed quite pleased. He bragged that Shi would 'get his.'" She shuffled around again. "I'm not sure what that meant."

Xiang-hua tucked away Jade's revelations. These plans certainly implicated Yao-sheng in a plot to take revenge on herbalist Shi. But what did that have to do with the murder victim? Had Yao-sheng hired the gangster only to kill him and frame Shi?

CHAPTER 23

Surrounded by books and a stack of rice paper, Shu-chang sat at his table—as he often did—preparing for the last hurdle in his father's dream: Shu-chang's passing the all-important, national exam. The gateway to his family's rise in prestige and status. Right now, that meant practicing writing pithy commentary on a Confucian text.

"Are you busy?"

The tentative voice brought him back to the bare classroom. Xiang-hua and Xiao-ren were peering through the door. Their faces glowed with excitement.

"No," he lied. He treasured this precious time when he could be lost in his studies. Nevertheless, he paused with his brush in mid-air and turned toward the invaders.

"Wait until you hear what we've discovered," Xiao-ren blurted out, striding into the room. "We were able to talk to several women this afternoon. Boy, it'd be hard to hide information from them. What a gossip network they have."

Shu-chang would have been skeptical—it was not unusual for Xiao-ren to exaggerate—but then he glanced at Xiang-hua and saw that she also looked pleased. He dropped his

174

brush on the blue and white porcelain dish; it rolled off and landed on his paper. A black dot spread over his freshly written characters. He groaned, picked up the errant brush, and hung it in his wooden brush holder.

Now he could give the brother and sister his complete attention.

Xiang-hua began a review of their findings from their visit to the warren. "The victim's name is Luo Yuan-jue. He was a northerner and had only been living in the Shou neighborhood for a few months. According to his landlady, he worked for He Da at the Flying Crane. But a couple of weeks ago, he picked up a side job with Yao-sheng."

Shu-chang sat up when he heard her mention He Da. Was there a relationship between picking up some extra money with Yao-sheng and his working for the gang leader? "Did she say anything about his being a gangster?" Shu-chang asked.

Xiang-hua shook her head. "From the beginning, she took it for granted that we knew he was a gang member and didn't have much to say about that. I must say that overall, we found her to be very forthcoming. Plus, she identified another fellow our victim hung around with."

"That guy rents a room from another widow friend of hers," Xiao-ren broke in.

"Who introduced us to Luo's sidekick's landlady. And that woman told us about discussions she'd heard among Luo's friends. Apparently, they didn't know who killed Luo or why, but they were trying to find out. His friends wanted revenge."

"Is it possible they were the thugs who tried to scare you off from your investigation?"

Shu-chang shrugged his shoulders. "Why? Wouldn't they want me to find the killer?"

Xiang-hua shifted her gaze into the middle distance as she thought about his question. "It's the Shou neighborhood's code," she finally answered. "They take care of their own.

They saw you as an arm of the court. If you found the guilty man and he was wealthy, he could easily escape punishment. If they found the murderer, no amount of money would save him from their revenge."

Xiao-ren nodded in agreement. "It was a matter of honor. They had to try to stop you."

Impressed with what they'd been able to discover, Shu-chang clasped his hands together and supported his chin as he took a moment to consider their findings. Xiang-hua always impressed him with her analytical abilities, but now he was beginning to appreciate her skills in developing trusting relationships with apparent strangers. She was unlike any woman he'd ever known. He glanced up at her. They made a good team. But did she feel the same?

Xiao-ren shuffled impatiently, bringing Shu-chang's thoughts back to the discussion.

"Well, now we have a name. But, if what the landlady told you is true, we won't find our killer in the neighborhood." Shu-chang frowned.

Xiao-ren grinned. "Wait till you hear the rest. What we found out after visiting Joyful Garden." He winked at Shu-chang.

"Joyful Garden? You went to a brothel? Why did you go there?" Shu-chang grimaced. *Would this woman never behave properly? Being friendly with strangers didn't include prostitutes.* He should never have agreed to her going to Shou Road in the first place.

"I am familiar with one of the ladies there. My grand-mother treated her," Xiang-hua said, clipping every word. She took a breath and continued: "Turns out, they know Yao-sheng very well. He has a favorite prostitute at Joyful Garden and he talks a lot. He did mention being heavily in debt and being very troubled by it."

Shu-chang shifted in his chair. Xiang-hua sat back,

watching him. Xiao-ren, elbows on the table, bent forward. His eyes shot back and forth between his sister and Shu-chang.

"Intriguing. What you discovered from the landlady reinforces an important piece of the puzzle," Shu-chang said, putting aside his judgmental thoughts about Xiang-hua's involvement with prostitutes. "We're getting overlapping information and that's good. The men in the wine shop also indicated that the victim was a gang member. He had a protective tattoo on his arm and a white feather was found near his body. Both signs of being a gang member. And then there's that Fu amulet you found in his sleeve."

"Yes, but he's not the only one to have such a protective charm," Xiang-hua said.

"Right. That adds another dimension. The Taoist priest who sold him the amulet sold a similar talisman to farmer Huai-liang. He's had a lot of bad luck lately. We know he recently lost his wife and now has a motherless baby. He blames the herbalist because he believes Shi killed her through medical incompetence." Shu-chang raised his hand in frustration. "Nevertheless, we still don't know what this has to do with our victim."

"I don't understand why Huai-liang came to you for help. Doesn't that make him look guilty?" Xiao-ren asked.

Xiang-hua answered first. "He was afraid of being embroiled in the killing somehow—even though he claims to be innocent—and came to Shu-chang to petition the provincial courts. And," she turned toward Shu-chang, "didn't you meet him coming out of the temple after he'd appealed to the sacred courts for aid in this matter? That makes it look like Huai-liang must feel pretty guilty about something."

Shu-chang nodded. "He had a motive to try and hurt Shi. It is possible he was being proactive, trying to protect himself from being incriminated. It is hard to understand what he was thinking. Any involvement with the legal system would bankrupt a poor farmer. Even if he was innocent. Perhaps he hoped that by attacking first, he would appear more innocent. After all, he was seen in a violent argument with the victim near Shi's home."

"And then there's Fen-peng, Lady Jiang's jealous husband," Xiang-hua said.

"Yes. He was seen threatening Shi and has no alibi for that evening. But, again, how would that connect him with the dead man?" Shu-chang stroked his chin in thought.

"And what about Ms. Chen?" Xiang-hua said. "Her husband had been selling her favors to the herbalist. When he demanded more money, Shi said no, he couldn't pay that much. Yao-sheng was furious. Apparently, his gambling debts were due and he had to have the money. He forbade Ms. Chen from seeing the herbalist anymore."

"She wasn't able to give him an alibi for the night of the murder, either, was she?" Shu-chang asked, leaning forward.

"Ms. Chen said he was out all night. Only coming back home in the early morning," Xiang-hua said.

"How did she know that? She could have been sleeping when he returned," Xiao-ren asked. He shook his head and frowned.

Shu-chang glanced at him. He knew that sneaking in late, after the household was asleep, was something his young cousin was familiar with.

"When he returned, he woke her and demanded she cook some rice. She usually rose before him, when it was still dark outside to make his morning meal. So, this was unusual. Much earlier than their everyday routine."

"Maybe he had business to take care of and needed to eat sooner," Xiao-ren said.

"The rice wasn't for him. He put it on their doorstep for the hungry ghosts."

"Yes. I noticed a dish outside the door," Shu-chang said. "Plus, a passing peddler saw Yao-sheng put it outside very early in the morning."

"The trouble is, all this again points to why someone might want to hurt Shi. It doesn't tell us anything more about our victim," Xiang-hua said. She paused and tapped her lips. "Jade at the Joyful Garden did say something that might be of interest. She told us about Yao-sheng being anxious and angry over his debts. It seems that although he had this large debt that he'd been having trouble paying off and was making him anxious, something changed. A few days ago, he suddenly became confident and calm. He bragged to her about having a perfect solution. Apparently, he'd found a resolution for his debt problem. Plus, he boasted that he'd expand his landholdings. Become a wealthy landowner."

"What was he going to do? It would have to be something big," Shu-chang said.

She gestured widely. "Unfortunately, I can't answer that. Jade is sure that somehow it involved destroying the herbalist and hiring Luo."

Shu-chang perked up. "Yao-sheng's plan could be to destroy herbalist Shi. If he became embroiled in a messy court case, that could ruin him. The dead man was found in his pigpen. He will certainly be dragged into court one way or the other. At minimum, he'll have to pay off countless numbers of lower court officials and even jailers." He slumped. "Still, I don't see how that would be of any monetary gain to Yao-sheng. Revenge, yes. But money?"

"We know that the victim had been hired as a handyman to work at Yao-sheng's house for a couple of days before his death. According to what we've found out, Ms. Chen's husband was specifically looking for an outsider, someone without family, as a short-term laborer. Why would he do that?" Xiang-hua's eyes brightened, and she shifted excitedly on her stool.

She answered her own question: "To have a victim no one would—"

"—particularly care about if they died in unusual circumstances," Shu-chang finished. "An anonymous victim whose body would be found in herbalist Shi's pen. What better way to create suspicion that Shi was somehow involved. There would be no evidence to prove otherwise. Not to mention that the magistrate has solved more than one case on circumstantial evidence alone. Shi could easily be convicted of murder. A perfect revenge scheme."

"Right. And we know that Yao-sheng was aware of the man's death before anyone found the body, because he did something that was completely out of character for him: He offered food early in the morning to a hungry ghost. An unhappy, dangerous ghost. A ghost of someone who died unexpectedly and who had no family to care for him in the afterlife," Shu-chang said.

"The victim's ghost," Xiang-hua finished.

A small smile played across Shu-chang's lips and he nodded.

"As soon as the court accused Shi of the murder, the town's people would raid his home and take everything. Yao-sheng among them." Xiang-hua went on. "Once convicted, his land would be confiscated and sold. And because a murdered man's body was found on the property, it would be difficult to sell. Who would take a chance on living on land that had the ghost of a murdered man on it? It would go very cheaply."

"But why would Yao-sheng want to buy the land if that's where he killed the herbalist?" Xiao-ren asked, bafflement etched on his crinkled forehead. "Wouldn't he have the same problem, only worse, if he actually was the murderer? Wouldn't the hungry ghost attack him?"

"Because he wasn't killed in the pigsty. He died elsewhere and his body was moved!" Xiang-hua said.

She looked to Shu-chang.

He took up her analysis. "Not enough blood in or around the pigpen for the murder to have been committed at the herbalist's place."

Now it was Xiang-hua's turn to nod her head in agreement.

"Then where?" Xiao-ren asked.

"Well, I did follow drag marks onto the road and initially thought they may have led to the warren," Shu-chang said, rubbing his chin.

"Oh, so he may have been killed in the Shou neighborhood. Is that what you think, Teacher?" Xiao-ren said, his face continued to be scrunched up as he puzzled it out. "Someone from there did him in after all."

Shu-chang shook his head. "Those drag marks were probably an attempt at misdirection. To make us look elsewhere. I believe the evil deed happened much closer than that."

Xiang-hua's hand sharply struck the table, causing her brother to jump at the sudden noise. "Yes. Our murderer did try to think of everything. Misdirection included. We need to pay the Yao-sheng household a visit." She looked at Shu-chang, whose eyes lit up. He nodded in agreement.

"It's time to bring justice to the victim and closure to the case," she said, rising from her chair.

CHAPTER 24

Before leaving, Shu-chang sent Xiao-ren to tell Zhong, Uncle Xin, farmer Huai-liang, and Chu to meet them at Shi's house. There, they would also gather up the herbalist and continue on to Yao-sheng's home next door.

Shu-chang and Xiang-hua immediately set out for the neighbor's house. Before proceeding to the door and announcing themselves, they stopped to inspect the enclosed yard. A couple of chickens started over to them, their heads ducking and bobbing. Always hungry, they automatically approached to see if a handful of grain might be thrown out into the yard.

Xiao-ren and the others finally arrived. In a cocoon of silent expectancy, they caught up with them as they waited outside the enclosure.

Once they'd all assembled, Xiang-hua was ready. She had a handful of seeds in a small bag hanging from her waist and threw them out toward the opposite side of the yard. The chickens rushed over and quietly pecked at the bounty.

Now that the chickens were occupied, they entered the

yard. Ms. Chen answered Shu-chang's knock. She didn't seem surprised to see the group standing before her.

"Who's there?" Yao-sheng yelled from within the dim interior.

"We're here to discuss the murder of Luo Yuan-jue," Shu-chang answered. Xiang-hua had advised him earlier that the room was too small to hold all of them, so he added, "Come outside and join us. You too, Ms. Chen."

Husband and wife joined the contingent in the yard. Yao-sheng looked disheveled, as if he'd just awakened, and his breath still smelled of stale liquor. Nevertheless, he marched out, defiance in the set of his jaw and lower lip. His wife stood behind, barely outside of the doorway. Her rolled sleeves revealed firm forearms and hands that grasped at the sides of her sullied, indigo overblouse.

"Why are you here bothering me?" Yao-sheng demanded. He poked a finger toward the herbalist. "He's your killer. The murdered victim was found in his yard, being eaten by his sow. What more do you want?"

Shi thrust his chin out, raised his hands, and started to move forward. "Why you—"

Zhong threw his arm up between the two men. "Stop!"

As if halted by an external force, both stood for a moment, pugnaciously staring at the other. Finally, just as Shu-chang thought he'd have to intervene physically, the two relented and stepped back.

"It's time to resolve this case and bring justice for Luo Yuan-jue," Shu-chang said. He and Xiang-hua laid out their findings, each reporting on what their investigations had revealed: who the murder victim was, his gang affiliation, his working for Yao-sheng, the arguments between Shi and Huai-liang, and Fen-peng's obsession with Shi. They included Yao-sheng pimping his wife and trying to sell her as a concubine.

To the latter, Yao-sheng guffawed. "What I do with my

P.A. DE VOE

wife is none of your business. Besides, all you're saying is that Shi should be dead and not that worthless gangster. Karma. Bad fate for the dead guy. That's all. I don't know what you're trying to do with this story. It certainly doesn't have much to do with us," he said, waving a hand at his wife. She kept her eyes glued to the ground, never looking up as he carried on.

"There's more," Shu-chang said and nodded to Xiang-hua, who picked up the story's thread.

"One key to the puzzle was your feeding the murdered man's ghost," she said.

"So what?" Yao-sheng asked. He nervously glanced over at Shi's pigpen. "It's common practice. Everyone feeds the wandering, hungry ghosts. Nothing unusual in that. That fellow died so close to my house, I had to feed him. Otherwise, who knows what could happen?" His eyes took on a haunted look as he glanced over at the spot where the corpse was discovered.

"It's something you've never done before. Never. You always claimed you didn't believe in such supernatural 'nonsense,'" Xiang-hua persisted. "Yet, on that day you came home early—very early—in the morning and insisted on having ghost rice prepared."

"What did you tell them? Are you an idiot?" Yao-sheng glared at his wife.

She didn't meet his gaze. She continued to stare at the ground, while her white knuckled hands grasped her long shirt.

"Prepared for a ghost of a man you insisted you didn't know was dead at the time," Shu-chang added. "And in the yard of a man you wanted to take revenge on."

Yao-sheng's shoulders sagged. His bluster dissolved. "Yes, I knew he had been killed. But I didn't do it." The words came pouring out of him. "I went to Joyful Garden that night and came home later than usual. Yuan-jue was supposed to meet me and to help me steal Shi's pig that night. It would bring a nice string of copper coins." He almost grinned as he shifted into boasting of his plans. But then he seemed to reassess. "I got back late, as I said. Yuan-jue wasn't around. And that pig was making so much noise." He wiped the sweat beads glistening on his forehead. "That's when I saw him on the ground, and the pig eating him. It made me sick."

"Yet you didn't try to do anything?" Shu-chang asked.

A shade of Yao-sheng's belligerence slipped back. "It was too late. He was obviously dead." He wiped his forehead again. "No sense in my getting involved."

"But you did get involved, didn't you?" Shu-chang went on. "You created those drag marks going out toward the road. Making it look like he'd been moved."

Yao-sheng gave him a sour look. "If I hadn't, people might think I was involved. He died right next door." His voice rose in pitch. "But, I didn't do it!"

Shu-chang and Xiang-hua looked at each other, and she went on.

"No. Not you," Xiang-hua said and shifted to the figure behind him. " Ms. Chen," her voice softened slightly, remembering all she had learned about the young woman's life. "You know it isn't your husband because you were the one to kill Yuan-jue. You planted his body at the herbalist's." She reached into her sleeve and took out a small, torn blue piece of fabric. "I believe we'll find this matches that mended section of your shirt's hem."

Ms. Chen's head jerked up. Her panicked eyes moved rapidly from one accuser to the other. She threw her hands up to push away the recrimination. "How could it be me? Why would I kill a man I don't know?"

"You did know him. He did work around the house for your husband. You said he never came inside, but he did. Your neighbor across the street saw him. Saw him enter your home on more than one occasion. Your husband sold your favors to him in return for fixing his house and surrounding wall. Isn't that so?" Shu-chang said. As sorry as he felt for her —for her being betrayed and abused by her husband—he had to push ahead in order to reinstate moral harmony.

"Yes. My husband," she spit out the word, "sold me like used property."

"And you knew things were about to get worse. He was planning on selling you off as a concubine," Xiang-hua said. She opened her hands out in a gesture of understanding. "At the same time, you believed Shi would save you from all that. By poisoning your husband."

Ms. Chen stood rooted to the spot, unable to move.

"But he didn't, did he? You began to think you'd been abandoned. Abandoned by the one person you thought you could trust. The one person you thought cared for you. So, you created your own revenge scheme. Kill Yuan-jue, who was a nobody as far as you were concerned, and put his body in Shi's pigpen."

At that, Ms. Chen's head snapped up. "How could I, a woman, move a dead man? Much less dump him on the other side of the pen's wall?"

Xiang-hua nodded. "That's what threw us off at first. We assumed the killer was a man. Our mistake. You're young and healthy. And, while working in the fields is difficult, it also made you strong. Strong enough to move Yuan-jue's body and push it over the wall. All the time you knew we would be looking for a man, someone who knew the victim and Shi, as well. You hoped that people would suspect your husband and implicate him because he'd been bragging loudly to anyone who would listen about how he was going to get revenge on Shi. Isn't that right?"

Crying, Ms. Chen slumped against the wall. "I hadn't planned to kill Luo, but he tried to take me. I pushed him away, telling him I'd report him to my husband. He just laughed and said my husband wouldn't care. I was nothing. In our struggle, he fell to his knees. I grabbed a knife and stabbed him in the back. It seemed like fate. As he died at my feet, I realized that his death was my chance to take revenge." She looked around her with hollow eyes.

Mouth agape, Yao-sheng stared at his young wife.

"What will happen to Ms. Chen and her husband?" Xiao-ren asked once they were all back in the classroom.

"Well, she killed one person and tried to blame another for the death. For that, the law is quite harsh. Especially since that other person was her husband," Shu-chang said. "She committed a crime against the moral order, and that is even greater than the original murder." He shook his head at the very thought.

"But Yao-sheng also broke the law by prostituting his wife —and that's against the moral order, too. Won't she get a diminished sentence since Yao-sheng abused her? And by law isn't he more accountable for her crimes than she is herself— since as her husband he is responsible for her behavior?" Xiao-ren asked again.

Chu scowled at his son's continued questioning, but Shu-chang answered without remarking on his forwardness.

"The fact that her husband mistreated her does not mitigate her crimes in any way. She will be shown no mercy and will be executed. And, while Yao-sheng was not involved in the murder, he did, as you say, prostitute his wife. Therefore, he will be charged for a crime against the moral order. His punishment is likely to be a beating of one hundred strokes with a heavy stick."

"Which could very well kill him as well," Xiang-hua noted. "Not many men can survive such a punishment."

"Unless he manages to bribe the jailer to not beat him mercilessly. Still, he'll very likely suffer serious injuries and may be crippled," Uncle Xin added. "That is probably what will happen. Although it means he'll have to sell all of his property to get enough money for the bribe."

"Ironic that his greed will lead to his impoverishment," Xiang-hua noted with a small shake of her head.

"Well, I heard Huai-liang was satisfied with all this, too," Xiao-ren went on. "Shi was arrested for adultery with a married woman, and the penalty for such a crime is ninety blows with a heavy stick. So, Huai-liang has been going around telling people that this proves the power of the gods to handle evil and evil doers. He's convinced the herbalist's punishment includes his malpractice in killing his wife. I heard he's giving a big dinner in honor of the gods as a thank you."

"And what about Lady Jiang's husband, Fen-peng?" Uncle Xin asked. "Has anyone heard about him?"

Xiang-hua's father nodded: "Fortunately, he never actually attacked the herbalist. Zhong believes Fen-peng's threats were all empty swagger and that he is incapable of real violence, so the security team leader will not bring charges against Lady Jiang's husband. His name will not be mentioned in the case."

"I saw him yesterday at an intimate gathering with some friends. He composed a poem about Lady Jiang, and her untouchable perfection as daughter-in-law and wife. We all thought it was one of his best poems." Uncle Xin smiled at the remembrance.

Shu-chang's gaze kept going back to Xiang-hua, who seemed to have withdrawn. She sat staring at her hands entwined in her lap, her expression pensive. "What's bothering you, cousin? We solved the murder. Luo Yuan-jue will get justice. His spirit can rest."

She leaned back into her chair and looked up with darkened eyes. "Ms. Chen was born into a world that gave no hope, no chance for a better life. It had nothing to do with her abilities, whatever they might be. How different from my own circumstances. What would my life be like without the family I, fortunately, was born into?" She cast a long, grateful gaze at her father and then went on. "I wonder if we are ruled by fate after all. Do we really have control over our lives? Over our futures? Even our future lives? Is it all predetermined after all?

A thoughtful silence spread over the others. Shu-chang's chest constricted. Karma. What role indeed did it play in their lives? Was it karma that brought him here to live with his mother's people, to meet Xiang-hua, a woman who constantly baffled and challenged him? What would his father say about such a brilliant, engaging, but forthright, woman? Would he have considered her a good daughter-in-law? The direction of his thoughts almost made Shu-chang blush. He quickly retreated from them.

Nevertheless, Xiang-hua's words once more crowded into his thinking. His life flashed before him. His father's and uncle's fates. Their sudden, violent deaths. Their unsatisfied spirits seeking justice. As the only male heir, it was his filial duty to bring them peace. Yet, he was beginning to wonder about his own fate in pursuing justice: was he to find it for others while his own family's murderers went free? He shook his head. Impossible.

THE END

CHARACTERS WITH PRONUNCIATION & DESCRIPTION

Character names in **No Way To Die** are spelled according to the Pinyin romanization system. The following list gives both the Pinyin spelling and suggested approximations of how the words might sound to an American speaker.

Xin Clan

Xin = *Shin*

Includes all people related by blood through the paternal, Xin, side of the family; all share the Xin surname; minority clan in town of Jian

Gao Clan

Gao = *Gaow*

Includes all people related by blood through their paternal, Gao, side of the family; all have Gao surname; largest and dominant clan in town of Jian

Hong Shu-chang

Hong Shu-chang = *Hong Shoe-chang*

Itinerant scholar; related to Xin clan through his mother

Jin-fang
> Shu-chang's friend from his home village

Uncle Xin
> Xin = *Shin*
> Shu-chang's mother's brother

Aunt Nu-er
> Nu-er = *New-air*
> Shu-chang's aunt, married to Uncle Xin

Xin Xiang-hua
> Xiang-hua = *Sheeang-whoa*
> Second cousin to Shu-chang on his mother's side of the family; sometimes called by the honorific "Sister"

Xin Xiao-ren
> Xiao-ren = *Sheeao-wren*
> Xiang-hua's younger brother; cousin to Shu-chang on his mother's side

Xin Chu
> Uncle Xin's cousin on his paternal side; father to Xiang-hua and Xiao-ren

Grandmother Yi-po
> Yi-po = *Ee-poe*
> Xiang-hua's paternal grandmother; a medical doctor specializing in working with female patients

Master Gao Zhong
> Gao Zhong = *Gaow Jong*
> Village security team leader

Granny Ao-po
> A widowed, older woman; midwife and coroner

Gao Shi
> Herbalist; victim found in his pigpen

Gao Yao-sheng
> Lives next door to Gao Shi, the herbalist

Ms. Chen
> Young wife to Gao Yao-sheng

Yan-du
> Taoist priest

Xin Fen-peng
> Lady Jiang's husband

Lady Jiang
> Jiang = *Geeang*
> Wife to Xin Fen-peng; cares for her mother-in-law

Gao Huai-liang
> Huai-liang = *Whai-liang*
> Poor farmer

Zhou
> Zhou = *Jo*
> Migrant laborer from Fuzhou City, Fujian Province; Shu-chang's friend

Lin
> Lin = *Lynn*

Migrant laborer from Fuzhou City, Fujian Province; Shu-chang's friend

Fang

Migrant laborer from Fuzhou City, Fujian Province; Shu-chang's friend

He Da

He Da = *Huh Da*

Gang member

Widow Yang

Luo Yuan-jue's landlady; lives in the Shou neighborhood

Granny Yueh

Bai-hong's landlady; lives in the Shou neighborhood

Bai-hong

Friend of the victim

Jade

Works at Joyful Garden; former patient of Xiang-hua's grandmother

Pearl

Works at Joyful Garden

Luo Yuan-jue

Victim found dead in pigpen

NOTES

The Ming Dynasty Mystery series tells stories of what it might have been like living during the late fourteenth century in southern China. I take cultural elements and weave their possible ramifications into the daily lives of my characters. In **No Way to Die**, for instance, the concept of karma—the belief in the interconnectedness of our past, present, and future lives—affects people differently, depending on their level of acceptance of this spiritual concept. And then there is their response to karma's impact on their lives: to struggle against it; to lead an honorable life in order to improve their future; or to capitulate to whatever happens in their present, believing all attempts at changing things would be useless.

Below are other cultural elements that existed in people's socio-cultural environment and had an impact on the characters in **No Way to Die**.

Gegu

Gegu involves cutting a piece of flesh from the arm or thigh, cooking it in a broth, and feeding it as medicine for a close family member. The practice has a long tradition, going back as far as the mid-700s, and was considered an act of filial piety. There was considerable controversy over the acceptability of such an act. For example, in 1394 the Emperor honored three people who committed gegu, but the next year he banned the practice. Nevertheless, women who committed gegu for their parents or in-laws continued to be memorialized in local gazetteers. This was a long-standing practice and, while normally marring one's own body in any way was considered unfilial, gegu was thought to be an honorable, Confucian act by some.

While none of the characters in **No Way to Die** were real people, they are sometimes inspired by actual, historical people. Lady Jiang, for instance, is based on a woman from the seventeenth century named Ji Xian. Ji Xian was both exceptionally filial and deeply spiritual, which led her to take the extraordinary step of committing gegu for members of her family. Her religiosity also opened her up to a psychic encounter with the deity Lord Guan, who enlightened her about her karmic burden.

For more on this, see:

Fong, Grace S. "'Record of Past Karma' by Ji Xian (1614-1683)," translated by Grace S. Fong. *Under Confucian Eyes*, edited by Susan Mann and Yu-yin Cheng. University of California Press, 2001.

Yu, Jimmy. "Nourishing the Parent with One's Own Flesh." *Sanctity and Self-Inflicted Violence in Chinese Religions 1500-1700*. Oxford University Press, 2012.

Marriage and Family Structure

Chinese family patterns were patrilineal, meaning people traced their family line through their father's side only, and patrilocal, meaning that when couples married they would, ideally, live with the husband's parents. The mother's side of the family was important in their extended network, but were designated as "outside" relatives; that is, outside of the patrilineal line.

It was incestuous for cousins related on the patrilineal side of the family to marry. However, a cousin from the mother's side—the matrilineal side—was considered a perfect marriage partner. While families could, and did, choose their children's spouses with other goals in mind—such as tying two wealthy families together or two medical families together—maternal cousins remained a popular marriage choice.

Coroners

"Grannies" was a term used for an eclectic group of women. They performed many needed roles, such as midwives, healers, matchmakers, caretakers for wealthy women, and coroners. A granny who worked as a coroner was known as *ao po* (which is the name I used for the granny in **No Way To Die**) and served within the civil government offices. She was called upon whenever there was a suspicious death. Although it was not her job to analyze the cause of death, as I had Xiang-hua do in this story, granny ao po was the one to handle the body when it was officially inspected— turning it over or lifting a limb. Typically, these grannies were older since their work involved intimately touching the corpse of a man or a woman. This type of work was considered lowly indeed.

For more on various types of Grannies and their work see:

Cass, Victoria. *Dangerous Women, Warriors, Grannies and Geishas of the Ming*. Rowman & Littlefield Publishers, 1999.

Court Use of Torture

Chinese law detailed what constituted a specific criminal act and the appropriate punishment for committing that particular crime. The basis for the law was a moral code which tied human behavior, the natural world, and the supernatural order together. Immoral and illicit behavior disrupted the balance among them, bringing about chaos and natural disasters. As a result, criminals had to confess and take responsibility for their actions to restore human and spiritual harmony. For serious crimes, the perpetrator could not be condemned until he confessed. At the same time, the court had a very short timeline to bring closure for any given criminal investigation. If the magistrate did not meet the court's designated timeline, the case could not be closed, and the magistrate would be severely punished for not fulfilling his duty to bring justice and re-establish harmony in a timely manner. Therefore, to pressure recalcitrant criminals, the government expected judicial torture to be applied to obtain confessions. The law clearly laid out what judicial torture techniques could be used and how they varied depending on such factors as age, sex, and social status of the individual.

Every staff member of the court system—and this included the scribes and yamen runners who carried messages —expected a "gift" from any person involved in a case. It also included the jailers, who oversaw the day-to-day well-being of those arrested and who, at times, also tortured their charges. As a result, being involved with the legal system could easily lead to economic disaster for a family.

Just being accused and arrested for murder could result in severe economic loss, for often neighbors and the general public would, upon hearing of the arrest, rush to the accused's property and steal whatever they could. This practice was so common that the magistrate Huang Liu-hung wrote about the need to control such rampant thievery.

For more on Ming law, go to:

Yonglin, Jiang, translator. *The Great Ming Code*. University of Washington Press, 2014.

For a look at the inner workings of a magistrate's life, see:

Liu-hung, Huang. *A Complete Book Concerning Happiness and Benevolence*, translated and edited by Djang Chu. The University of Arizona Press, 1984.

ACKNOWLEDGMENTS

Writing a novel is a solitary task involving long hours at the computer as well as doing research. However, a story's final version often benefits from the input of others. **No Way to Die** is no exception. First, the cover benefited greatly from Kelly Cochran's creative input. Thank you, Kelly. I would also like to thank my wonderful beta readers, Christina Juelfs and Linda Harris Dobkins (AKA Jo Allison), for their insightful comments. A fresh set of eyes is always a plus. And, as ever, I owe a debt of gratitude to both my excellent editor, Renèe DeVoe Mertz, and my observant husband. Thank you all.

OTHER MING DYNASTY MYSTERIES & ADVENTURES BY P.A. DE VOE

Deadly Relations,
A Ming Dynasty Mystery

The Mei-hua Trilogy,
a box set (e-book)
Hidden,
A Mei-hua Adventure
Warned,
A Mei-hua Adventure
Trapped,
A Mei-hua Adventure
Lotus Shoes,
a Mei-hua short story

Judge Lu short stories,
From Judge Lu's Ming Dynasty Case Files

To discover more stories
about Imperial China, visit: **padevoe.com**

If you enjoyed **No Way to Die**, I would appreciate your leaving a short review on the site where you bought the book. Your review will make a difference in helping other readers find early Ming Dynasty mysteries.

Thank you!

www.ingramcontent.com/pod-product-compliance
Lightning Source LLC
Chambersburg PA
CBHW031417250626
47155CB00004B/1526

* 9 7 8 1 9 4 2 6 6 7 1 1 7 *